SPY
FACTORY

My School is a Spy Factory

STEVEN STICKLER

Word Conspiracy Press
Portland, Oregon

CONTENTS

PROLOGUE

1903, New York City

The supervisor and his assistant walked through a tunnel, deep beneath the city, along a narrow path that wound through piles of debris. They moved at a rapid pace, weighed down by heavy packs that held digging equipment and supplies. The young assistant carried a faint lantern that created large shadows against the concrete walls and ceiling. The air remained dusty from the morning's work and the smell of dust and dynamite lingered from the day's explosions further up the tunnel.

They had been working like this for the last twenty nights, and each could feel it in his tired legs and dull senses.

The supervisor checked the notes he had scribbled on an envelope earlier in the day. "Quickly, we are almost there."

His assistant nodded. He knew the importance of speed. They had much work left to do, and they couldn't afford to be caught doing it.

"There," said the supervisor as he pointed to the tunnel wall to their right. "Right there. It should be only three more steps and on that wall. Look for the triangle."

The perspiration on the assistant's forehead glistened in the dim light as he bent over and held the lantern against the wall. He ran his hand slowly across the cold concrete until his gaze rested on a small triangle etched in the concrete at about waist height. "Here it is."

The supervisor bent over and rested his hands on the knees of his dark blue overalls as he examined the wall. "Yes, this is it sure enough," he said as he checked his notes again. He placed his hands against the wall to mark an area two feet across. "From here to here. We'll need the chisels."

They began working immediately, knowing they had little time to waste. The sound of the hammer against the chisel reverberated through the entire length of the tunnel as they slowly chipped away at the concrete. In minutes, they had created an area that was large enough to crawl through, but only a foot deep.

Every so often they stopped so the assistant could take the lantern and walk a short distance up the tunnel on either side, checking to make sure they didn't have company. It was part of the training. They knew that they could never be too careful.

They continued to chip away until the chisel poked through the wall and fell with a clatter on the other side.

They had reached the target.

It took only a few minutes to finish the job. They chiseled until there was a hole in the wall large enough to crawl through, and then they smoothed the sides of the hole to prevent injury.

"Hand me the lantern," instructed the supervisor as he reached out his hand.

On his hands and knees, he crawled far enough to poke his head and arm through the opening. He slowly lifted the lantern and held it in the space on the other side of the wall, then watched the flame flicker as a breeze passed through.

He looked one way and then the other, marveling for only a moment at what he saw. Then he grasped the chisel that had fallen to the ground. Stretching to reach further into the space on the other side of the opening, he used the chisel to mark a small triangle on the wet clay soil.

Once the triangle was deep enough, he pulled a small metal tin from his pocket and opened it. The powder inside sparkled brightly in the lantern light. He sprinkled some powder into the outlines of the triangle until it glowed like a neon sign in the darkness.

When he was finished, he backed out of the opening and placed the lantern gently on the ground.

"Okay, that does it," he said firmly. "Now we need to cover it up."

The assistant didn't ask questions. It seemed the obvious thing to do.

They began unpacking the materials. Most of what they needed had been prepared in advance. The false panel, the hinges, and the locking mechanism were ready. They simply needed to mix the plaster and match the paint.

After less than an hour of work, they stepped back and examined the wall.

"Perfect," said the supervisor as he held the lantern against the wall. There was no sign of the opening they had created. The entire area looked exactly like the rest of the tunnel wall, part of a vast expanse of uneven concrete, like an old sidewalk running along a vertical wall.

The assistant scattered debris to cover the area where they had been working.

"Very good," said the supervisor, checking his watch in the dim light. "We are on schedule. We have two more to complete tonight before the work crews start in the morning. We can't be down here when they get here."

They picked up their packs, lighter now than when they had arrived, and continued walking up the tunnel as their shadows danced on the walls and ceiling.

"Do you really think they'll ever need to use these?" The assistant brushed concrete dust off his chest and shoulders.

"Well, I don't know the answer to that," replied the supervisor uncertainly. But as he looked up at the tunnel narrowing in front of them, the walls at one point not much wider than a subway car, the confidence returned to his voice. "But, yes, yes, I suppose they might."

Of course, he didn't know one way or the other. But he couldn't let his assistant know that. The young man needed confidence, after all.

All that the supervisor knew—all he *needed* to know, for that matter—was that the plan rested on what they were doing. They couldn't fail, or the plan would fail. That was enough to keep him going.

1. THE SECRET

Present day, New York City

When they asked me in grade school what I wanted to be when I grew up, I gave a long list of answers.

I said I wanted to be a surgeon.

I said I wanted to be an architect.

I said I wanted to be an archaeologist.

One year, I even said I wanted to be President of the United States.

Not once did I say I wanted to be a spy. Or a secret agent. Or basically anyone who battled the forces of evil to save the world.

I figured I would leave that to people who actually, you know, enjoyed danger. Sneaking around, cracking codes, chasing bad guys, and performing ninja moves weren't for me. I was a simple kid, and I planned to spend my life doing something safe and predictable.

But someone else—someone I had never met—had a different plan.

And so, on an otherwise ordinary September evening, on the eve of my first day of middle school, a single phone call changed my life forever.

I have often wondered what would have happened if Mom hadn't answered the phone. What if we had been out for pizza and arrived home late? What if we had been in the middle of family game night and let the call go to voice mail? What if Dad had been on a conference call—the way he often was—and had ignored the insistent beep of call waiting?

Had any of those things happened, I never would've known about the Institute, and I certainly never would've learned The Secret.

But we weren't out for pizza.

It wasn't family game night.

Dad wasn't talking on the phone.

It was the last day of summer vacation, and there were too many things to do. There were pencils to sharpen, notebooks to label, and lunches to make.

And, it turned out, there were mysterious phone calls to answer.

I could tell the call was serious when Mom motioned for Dad to listen in. They shared one receiver, listening intently, with their heads so close together that it looked as if they were attached. They asked only a few hushed questions, too quietly for me to hear from where I lay sprawled among school supplies scattered across the living room floor. But I could see the concern on their faces and hear the worry in both their voices.

Next was the talk. They sat me down in my favorite red chair, the one with the smooth fabric that was so old that it was frayed at the seams.

"Nate," began Mom, in her most sympathetic, prepare-to-hear-something-you-won't-like tone, "we have been talking to someone from the school district and, well, some other folks … "

Her voice trailed off as she looked over at Dad, inviting him to continue. That was usually the way it worked in situations like this. She would start, and he would finish. They were like partners that way. Any time they partnered up like that, I braced myself for bad news.

"Yes, and we have some, uh, well, *exciting* news for you," Dad continued, latching onto the word "exciting" as if it were a lifeboat in a stormy ocean. "The school district has decided that there is a middle school across town that would be a perfect fit for you. It's called the Benjamin Tallmadge Institute, and it sounds like, well, an *exciting* opportunity. Much better than JFK. You'll love it."

I wanted to protest. Questions bounced around in my brain like popcorn in a popcorn popper. *What about all my friends? What about the fact that, you know, I actually toured JFK and I knew where all the classrooms were, and where my locker was, and the names of all the teachers? What about the fact that I had my classes memorized, my path between them mapped out and timed so I would never be late or get lost? What made this new school a "perfect fit" anyway? What did that even mean? And, finally, institute of what, exactly?*

There were so many questions that when I tried to convert them into something resembling an argument, I was left nearly speechless. All I could manage was a meek and helpless whisper. "Um, okay."

"It will be great," Mom said in the least convincing tone I had heard since the time our whole family— Mom, Dad, my little brother Charlie and I—all piled into the car for an eight-hour drive to visit Aunt Diane.

3

That trip, it turned out, wasn't great. It was the opposite of great. It was the longest eight hours of my life, in fact.

So with no discussion and no warning, my entire life was transformed. Everything I had imagined about my future in middle school was gone in an instant. There would be no sharing a locker with my best friend Austin; no roaming the halls I had visited dozens of times to, as the teachers all said, "ease the transition;" and, no short bus ride to school and back. All of it was gone, replaced by the uncertainty of attending a completely new school among kids I didn't know, crowded hallways I had never seen, and teachers who probably wouldn't even know my name.

Curious about my new school, I did what any kid would do: I Googled it. What did I find? Nothing. That's right, Nada. Zero. Zilch. Zippo. As far as Google was concerned, there was no such thing as the Benjamin Tallmadge Institute. There was no search result. No map. No web site. Not even a newspaper article. It wasn't even listed on the school district website. Apparently, unless you were one of the "lucky" few who end up transferred there on the last day of your otherwise glorious summer vacation, the Institute was invisible to you.

Nervous and excited at the same time, I snuggled into my reading tent and stared at the bed sheet that served as a ceiling. Nestled in the corner of my bedroom, with bed sheets for walls and large pillows for flooring, my reading tent was the most secure and comfortable place I knew. But on that night it didn't comfort me or relax me. Not one bit.

When we arrived at the school the next day, I shifted nervously in my seat, hoping one last time that it was all a dream. I even gave my leg a little pinch, but all that did was make my leg hurt.

"It will be a great school year," Dad said. He was always the optimist.

Charlie, sitting on the seat beside me, was different. He was optimistic, sure. But he usually got right to the point. He didn't sugarcoat things. His one simple comment, emerging from his mouth like a verbal sneeze, pretty much summed up the way I felt. "That place looks scary."

I didn't usually like to admit that Charlie was right. After all, I couldn't agree with him too often or he might lose respect for me. But this time I saw no point in disagreeing as I stepped out of the car. "Yep, scary is right."

The first day of school—especially at a new school—was always a little strange. There was the nervous anticipation of the unknown, the uncertainty about fitting in, and the practical issue of finding classrooms, lockers, and bathrooms.

This was different.

I could tell from the moment I climbed the steps to the entrance of the Institute that it wasn't like any school I (or probably you) had ever seen.

The first sign was the entrance. Eight doorways faced the wide marble stairway. Before each doorway was a single file line of students, each one appearing just as stunned as I was to be there. There was no jostling or arguing. Just the silent resignation of students who, it appeared, weren't all that anxious to improve their positions in line. They looked like ants lining up to enter an anthill haunted house.

Then there were the lights. Above each doorway were perched two lights: one green and one red. When the green light flashed, the door below opened and a single student entered. It was always the same routine. Green light: one student entered. Red light: all students waited. Green light: another student entered. Red light: all students waited.

When my turn came and the door closed behind me, I found myself in a small room with no other doors. It was like standing in an elevator, or maybe a closet. I was about to turn around and leave when a computerized voice began giving me instructions.

"Eyes closed," said the voice as the air in the room began to rush and swirl. I felt like I was standing in a vacuum cleaner.

"Eyes open," said the voice as a narrow beam of red light scanned across my eyes.

"Stand still," said the voice as a metal ring two feet across, the size of a hula hoop, lowered from the ceiling and dropped over the top of me, moving from my head to my feet and back up without ever touching me.

"Arms in front, palms up," said the voice. When I obeyed, a blue ray of light from the ceiling slowly scanned my palms.

"Welcome, Agent Nate Fischer," said the voice as I felt the floor begin to drop. I was in an elevator, moving to a lower floor. Then, within only a few seconds, the wall in front of me disappeared and I was standing before a large opening.

Agent Nate Fischer? I was sure there had been some sort of mistake. After all, did this computer honestly think I looked like the sort of kid who would be an agent? Maybe I could have looked like an insurance agent. Or perhaps an agent for professional soccer players. But somehow I got the feeling that wasn't the sort of agent this computer was talking about.

"Proceed to your station," was all the voice said.

The voice didn't say, "Welcome to our school!"

The voice didn't say, "Hope you enjoy your day!"

The voice didn't even mention what was on the lunch menu.

This computer was all business.

That was my introduction to my new middle school. It wasn't what I expected. I expected lockers, lousy cafeteria food, and maybe a few bullies. I didn't end up with any of those things. I ended up with elevator entrances and eye scanners before first period.

In a day full of surprises, nothing surprised me more than the first thing they told me during orientation.

That was when I learned The Secret. It happened before they even assigned me a locker.

There were maybe 20 of us sitting in an auditorium that had room for a few hundred. Everyone else seemed comfortable. I wasn't. The more I hunched down in my chair trying to be invisible, the more I felt like everyone was looking at me.

At the front of the room stood a man none of us had ever seen. It was clear from looking at him that he was important. He had that sort of look. With his white hair, penetrating eyes, and long face he reminded me immediately of the old and wise Obi-Wan Kenobi from *Episode IV*. At least, he looked the way Obi-Wan might have looked if Obi-Wan had dressed in loafers, jeans, and a bright green sweater.

"Greetings," said the Obi-Wan look-alike. "I am Poppleton."

He didn't call himself Professor Poppleton, or Principal Poppleton, or even Mister Poppleton. Just Poppleton. Still, it was clear from the way he said it that he was in charge.

"You're all smart enough to know that this is no ordinary middle school. In fact, I don't know that I would call it a middle school at all." He paused to let the meaning of his words sink in. "It has a different purpose. It will not prepare you to be teachers or architects or doctors or lawyers. Those are noble professions, but this school exists to train you for one thing and one thing only: to be spies."

The sound of gasps filled the auditorium. Some were gasps of shock. Others were gasps of conspiratorial intrigue. Mine was a gasp of *oh, man, what did Mom and Dad get me into?*

"That's right," Poppleton continued. "You are all spies-in-training. You see, we have been watching you. We have scouts in all the schools. Teachers, students, even janitors. They saw something in each one of you that they thought would make you great spies. Starting now, you are acting agents of the Benjamin Tallmadge Institute. You will undertake missions to keep our country safe. The missions won't be easy. If they were easy, we would leave them to the FBI or the CIA." He let out a little chuckle, the kind of chuckle you could tell came from a joke that he thought up 20 years ago and repeated at the start of every school year.

None of us chuckled. We were either shocked or scared or both.

Then his expression became serious and, in a hushed tone, he continued, "The most important thing to remember is that the existence of the Institute is a secret. Only current and former agents and the most senior officials in our government know what we do here. It has been that way since George Washington and Benjamin Tallmadge founded the Institute—"

Poppleton paused as curious whispers filled the room. "George Washington? Like *President* George Washington?" The questions were asked quietly, stranger to stranger, but Poppleton heard them all.

"Oh, yes, I mean *the* George Washington. He learned how important spy craft was during the Revolutionary War. Wouldn't have won without it. That's why he and his chief spy founded this place. Nothing more important than training spies. But back to my point. To the rest of the world, we are an ordinary, run-of-the-mill middle school. Nothing more. It is crucial that we keep it that way. Agents have died to keep this secret. Many more will die if we fail to keep it. Nobody can know what we actually do here. Not even your parents."

Anyway, that was how I learned The Secret: sitting in a mostly empty auditorium, deep underground, next to a bunch of nervous strangers.

Now, you might think that a school for spies sounds fun. After all, what sort of kid wouldn't want to live the exciting life of a secret agent?

Well, maybe a school for spies sounds fun to *you*. But it sure didn't sound fun to me. To me it sounded unpredictable and scary. You see, I was never the type of kid who sought adventure. I never wanted to be like Luke Skywalker, or Harry Potter, or even Frodo. I didn't wish to heroically battle the forces of evil. If I had been Luke Skywalker, I would have stayed on Tatooine. And if I had been Frodo, I definitely would have stayed in the Shire. I didn't wish for a life full of danger or action or even anything that could be accidentally mistaken for danger or action.

I wished for something else: to be at a normal middle school with my friends, with a predictable routine, and nothing unsafe at all. Math, humanities, science, art, lunch, music, and a few electives; playing with my friends before school; the scent of tater tots lingering in the hallways; waiting anxiously for the bell to ring. Nothing spy-like at all. Just the normal routine of an ordinary sixth grader.

But as I sat there in the auditorium with the details of The Secret still fresh in my ears, I knew that this other life, this normal life of a middle schooler, wasn't to be. My school wasn't normal and neither was my life.

That evening, as we sat around the dinner table, my parents asked the usual questions about my new school. They wanted to know what the kids were like, which teachers I had for my classes, and even what kind of food they served in the cafeteria. As Charlie looked up occasionally, with a light purple mustache of triple-berry smoothie across his upper lip, I told them as much as I could without revealing The Secret.

I told them about the classrooms and the teachers.

I told them about the other students.

I told them about Poppleton and the cafeteria food.

"Sounds like an interesting school," Dad said.

"Yeah, pretty normal, sounds like," Mom said.

Dad, I wanted to blurt out at the top of my lungs, *my school is not just interesting. And Mom, it definitely is not normal. Not even close. My school is a spy factory!*

2. THE MISSION

The day of my first mission started like every other day at the Institute.

First period. Codes class. Trying to crack an impossible code.

I nearly had it figured out when the mission assignment alert began blaring from the classroom speakers.

Beep. Beep. Beeeeeeep! Beep. Beep. Beeeeeeep!

When a mission assignment alert sounded at the Institute, everything else stopped. It was the most basic rule of our school day. That was because most of our missions were pretty urgent. Usually, they were life-or-death. They couldn't wait for us to finish our corn dogs at lunchtime or our attack moves in battle training. They couldn't even wait for us to finish cracking codes in Codes class.

So, along with every kid in our school, I headed to the auditorium for a mission assignment assembly.

We all knew what was coming. Poppleton would enter and describe a mission. Then, during a hushed silence, he would choose a lucky group of agents to complete it.

I scanned the room looking for my partner, Lucy. She was sitting in the front row, absent-mindedly twisting her hair with one of her hands while staring off into space as if she were watching a movie that no one else could see.

That was the thing about Lucy: she had many skills, but paying attention during an assembly wasn't one of them. Her mind tended to wander. I couldn't blame her, really. Assignments assembly could be pretty boring. But if there's one thing that an agent couldn't afford, it was a partner who wasn't paying attention during an assignment assembly. So I usually sat right next to her, poking her in the ribs every few minutes to keep her alert.

"Hey, are you awake yet?" I asked as I sat down next to her and gently snapped my fingers in front of her face.

"Huh? Oh! Yeah, just barely," she said. "What do you think the assignment is today? I heard it might be—"

Her voice cut off in mid-sentence as Poppleton walked to the front of the room and cleared his throat. He was holding the same coffee mug he always held. It was one of those mugs that had *World's Best Teacher* printed on it, except that in the space between *Best* and *Teacher*, someone had written the word *Spy* with bright red paint.

We always got a chuckle out of that mug. We didn't know whether he had received it as a gift or had made it himself. But just the mere possibility that he had made it himself—sitting at his desk with a paintbrush in one hand, carefully tracing out those three letters, then holding the mug out at arm's length to examine his work—was enough to make anyone chuckle.

"Okay, agents," Poppleton said in a stern voice. "Time to get serious. We have a Level One mission today."

A murmur of excitement spread throughout the room. A Level One was rare. Only the most urgent and important—not to mention dangerous—missions received a Level One designation. Every agent in that room wanted to be assigned to a Level One.

Every agent, that is, except for me. What I wanted was to return to Codes class and finish my code-cracking. I was anxious to go out on a mission, sure. That was what I had trained for. But a Level One for my first mission ever? That wasn't something I wanted. I preferred the idea of easing into the whole mission thing.

"Sorry, but this one is top secret, need-to-know basis only. I'll be assigning it to four agents. The rest of you will need to leave the room."

He took a sip from his coffee mug as every agent in the room leaned forward expectantly, hoping to hear his or her name called.

Well, almost every agent. Lucy didn't look excited at all. She wasn't even paying attention. She was focused on folding a scrap of paper she held on her lap. It was typical. Lucy spent most of her free time doing Origami and, at least as far as I could tell, she spent a lot of her class time doing it, too.

I had to admit that she was a master at it. Give her a scrap of paper—any scrap of paper—and she would fold it into a piece of art. Animals, cartoon characters, tiny ninja warriors, and enormous buildings. Yes, my partner Lucy was a self-described fold-nerd. And on this particular day, I could see, she was folding what remained of a Subway wrapper into the tiniest X-wing fighter I had ever seen.

I poked her hard in the ribs just as Poppleton announced our names.

"I need Nate and Lucy to stay here," Poppleton said. I jerked my head around to look at him as I heard my name. "Lenny and Isabel, you stay also. The rest of you please return to your classes. Oh, unless you are in Counter-Espionage class this period. In that case please head to the lab for a surprise test."

He paused as the rest of the agents filed out of the auditorium. I heard poorly-disguised groans and saw quite a few envious glances cast in our direction.

Frankly, I gladly would have given up my assignment and let someone else have a chance at glory. But it didn't work that way. We performed the missions we were assigned, no questions asked.

"Okay, let's get down to business," Poppleton said as he motioned for the four of us to join him next to the mission assignment table at the front of the room. "Lenny and Isabel will be leading the mission. Nate and Lucy will observe."

That was the way it worked. Sixth graders didn't lead missions. That was for seventh and eighth graders. We sixth graders just tagged along to learn the ropes. I didn't mind it so much. In fact, I was glad not to be leading the mission. Things could get pretty dangerous out there.

Except in this case, I wasn't so sure I trusted the eighth grader that would be leading the mission.

Lenny.

The thing about Lenny was that there seemed to be two versions of him. On the one hand, there was nice Lenny. He helped me figure out how to work my locker on the first day of school and never embarrassed me by telling people about it. He introduced me to some of the eighth graders as "one swell dude." And, on the day I accidentally wore my pants to school inside-out, he stood outside the bathroom door to keep people from coming in while I was changing them back to inside-in. That version of Lenny I liked.

On the other hand, there was mean Lenny. He once made fun of me for mispronouncing a word—a *hard* word—in Spanish class. He said negative things about other kids when they weren't around. And, if someone ever made the mistake of sharing a secret with him, he would broadcast it to the entire school. That version of Lenny I didn't like.

The problem with the two versions of Lenny was that I never knew which version I was going to get. It changed from day to day, and even hour to hour, and there was no Lenny clock or calendar telling me which version to expect. It made things unpredictable, and more than anything it made it hard to trust him.

Lucy felt the same way. We had talked about it. That was what partners did.

But I doubted that Poppleton was concerned with how Lucy and I felt about Lenny. He had more important things to think about, like the success of the mission. I assumed he had his reasons for choosing Lenny as one of the team leaders.

Of course, at that time, I didn't completely understand what those reasons were. I wouldn't figure that out until later. Had I known, I would have done everything differently.

"Okay, listen up agents. We have a lot to cover." Poppleton set his coffee mug on the table and looked up. "There's a threat to our security. We need to act quickly."

"Our security? You mean the country's security?" Isabel asked.

"Well, yes, eventually," Poppleton said. "But this involves the Institute directly. We are at grave risk. The Syndicate is involved."

My spine stiffened, and my eyes widened when he uttered those last four words. I had a hard enough time adjusting to the idea of a Level One mission, but the Syndicate being involved terrified me. It was a more secretive and mysterious organization than the Institute. Its agents were well-trained and every bit as smart and deadly as ours. In fact, the Syndicate was like the Institute in a lot of ways except for one: the Syndicate was evil.

I glanced over at Lucy, prepared to poke her in the ribs to remind her to pay attention. But there was no need. Poppleton had her full attention. Mentioning the Syndicate had that sort of effect, even on Lucy.

"They are after the list." Poppleton paused to let the information sink in. It took him about two seconds to realize that we had no idea what list he was talking about. "Oh, sorry, my apologies. Some background: we keep a list of all our agents, both current agents and former agents, along with their current addresses. Well, the Syndicate has been after that list for years, and—"

"Is that our mission, to guard it?" Lenny asked, interrupting Poppleton in mid-sentence, and with what seemed like a bit too much enthusiasm.

"Well, in a way I suppose. You see, we keep the list on the safest part of our computer system. We have always thought it was invulnerable to attack. But now we have evidence that it may be vulnerable."

"What sort of evidence?" Isabel asked. "Do you mean real intelligence? Like we have intercepted a Syndicate communication of some sort?"

"Well, I can't tell you how he found out, but an old friend of mine contacted me this morning to tell me about the threat. He is pretty sure someone at the Syndicate has figured out how to get to the list."

"But I thought we had the most powerful computers in the world," Isabel said, "and also the very best programmers and hackers. Surely the Syndicate is no match for that."

"Well, normally that would be true. And it has been true up until now." Poppleton paused as he slowly ran his fingers through his white hair. "But according to my friend, the Syndicate has developed some sort of secret computer code, like a virus that even we can't stop. Once they unleash it, it will spread through the Internet to almost every computer in the world. Within hours, they will control almost everything. Airports, stock exchanges, missile launch computers. Everything. And they will have a list of all our agents."

Lenny snorted. "So they will know my name? Big deal. Let them know my name. What are they going to do, send me a birthday card?"

Poppleton rolled his eyes and stared at Lenny for a moment. I suspected that he seriously regretted putting Lenny in charge of this mission. But he couldn't change his mind at that point. Once a set of agents started on a mission, they had to see it through. That was just the way it worked.

"Lenny," Poppleton said before pausing for emphasis, "it is far more serious than that. They don't care about your birthday. Maybe Nate or Lucy can explain the, uh, *finer* points of this?"

Lucy didn't hesitate. "Well, it seems pretty obvious to me. They aren't going to stop with just getting the list. They are going to use it for something."

"Exactly," I said, trying to think of a tactful way of explaining it without making Lenny feel foolish. "I'm guessing they would probably want to, you know, keep the Institute from stopping whatever plans they have after they take over the Internet. That could mean eliminating obstacles, like, I suppose—"

"They want to eliminate *us!*" Isabel said with a gasp. "That's why they want the list. They want to track down all our agents and capture them."

"Capture them or, I expect, kill them," I said, trying my best to sound brave even as I felt my voice quivering.

"I think that's a safe bet," Poppleton said. "And it might even be worse than that. You know, the Syndicate is pretty ruthless. They might not stop with eliminating

19

the agents. They might suspect the families, too. After all, they don't know how much the families have been told. Or at least they're not supposed to know."

I did all I could to look brave, but I certainly didn't feel brave. What I felt was a cold chill run down my spine, like that time bad Lenny stuffed a snowball down the back of my shirt. I knew, of course, that this was a dangerous job. But the fact that my family was at risk was a new one altogether.

I could tell Lucy, Lenny, and Isabel were thinking the same thing I was: this was suddenly very serious. Very serious, indeed.

Of course, it wasn't unusual for individual agents to face risks on their missions. We were used to that, and we trained for it. But for the entire fate of the Institute, the lives of other agents, and the very survival of our families to rest upon the success of our mission was a new feeling altogether.

"We need to stop them before they get that far. My friend has some information that will help us out. He needs us to come pick it up. It seems like a pretty simple mission, but he has warned me that there is danger involved. Enemy agents are looking for this information. You must be very careful."

"Where are we meeting him?" asked Lenny.

"Down at the University. His name is Professor Wilson, and he's at some sort of conference down there. Here." Poppleton handed Lenny a wrinkled scrap of paper with an address written on it. "You can take the Red Line to get there."

"Okay, let's go. Lockers first, then meet at Red Station."
Lenny was clearly pleased to be in charge.

"Yes, you all get going." Poppleton made a shooing motion with his arms. "Oh, but Nate, you wait here for a moment. I need to talk to you about something in private."

"Meet me at my locker," Lucy said as she left the room with the others.

Given the urgency of our mission, I was surprised that Poppleton asked me to stay. I thought perhaps he could sense my lack of enthusiasm and was planning to give me a pep talk. Maybe even a few pointers on Level One tactics. Or even a special gadget that would give me an advantage.

But he didn't give me a pep talk.

He didn't share any pointers.

And, unfortunately, he didn't give me a special gadget.

He had other things on his mind. Important things. Scary things. Things that, once I heard them, made me wish I wasn't an agent at all.

With the others gone, he whispered to me in a hushed voice. "Nate, I assigned you and Lucy to this mission for a reason. What you need to know—"

Poppleton paused in mid-sentence and held up his hand as if to stop me from speaking. Lenny had stepped back into the room. "Poppleton, do we need the full mission pack, or is this a light mission?"

"The full pack," said Poppleton. "There's nothing light about this mission. You need to get going; Red Station Chief is waiting."

"Okay, boss. We're on it." Lenny backed slowly out of the room, eying the two of us suspiciously. "Meet you at Red Station, Nate."

Poppleton remained silent for a moment after Lenny left. He looked at the doorway as if he suspected that Lenny may come barging back in at any moment. Finally, after what seemed like minutes, he inched closer to me until our faces were less than a foot apart.

"I can't tell you everything now. It isn't safe. And, I could be wrong. Oh, I very much hope I'm wrong," he said as he grasped my shoulders and gave a sort of pathetic, half-scared, half-nervous chuckle. "Let's just say that you need to be *extremely* careful on this mission, do you hear me? *Extremely* careful."

Poppleton was making me nervous. What was with the nervous chuckle? Why was he telling me to be *extremely* careful? Weren't we trained to be careful on all our missions? What made this mission any different? And, for that matter, didn't he know that I, of all people, was *always* extremely careful? After all, I was the guy who wore a life preserver to the school water-balloon fight. I was the guy who checked the Doppler radar before going outside every morning. I was the guy, maybe the only guy, who flossed in the morning *and* in the evening. And he was telling *me* to be careful?

"Yes, we'll be careful. We'll all be careful. Don't worry," I said.

"No, no, you don't understand," he said as his glance shifted to the doorway and back to me. "Let me put it this way. Nate, do you know what a break-the-glass moment is?"

I honestly had no idea what he was talking about. Why would anyone want to break the glass? It just seemed messy. And, you know, broken glass was sort of risky. I started to wonder if perhaps Poppleton was suffering some sort of mental breakdown. I hesitated, hoping that an answer would come to me. But nothing came. "Umm, no, I'm not so sure what you mean."

"It's okay, it's okay," Poppleton said emphatically as he waved a hand in the air. "It's just a phrase I use sometimes. It just means a moment of extreme danger. You know, the way those fire extinguishers in most buildings sit behind a piece of glass that says 'break glass in emergency'? That's where I got that phrase."

"Right." I wondered what this had to do with our mission or, for that matter, with anything. "That makes sense."

"Well, Nate, I worry that the Institute may be facing a break-the-glass moment. I'm going to give you this." He looked back at the doorway as if making sure no one was watching, then handed me a sealed envelope. "This is for you to keep to yourself. Open it only if you encounter a break-the-glass moment. That's when you'll need it. Let's just hope it doesn't come to that."

I placed the envelope in my pocket without even looking at it. My mind was already preoccupied with thoughts of the mission and of the dangers we would face. This certainly wasn't the way I thought a Level One mission would feel. I expected to feel exhilarated and brave. But instead I felt reluctant and scared.

More than anything, at that moment I wished I was back in Codes class, feeling the sense of accomplishment that would come from deciphering that tricky code. But it was too late for that. The mission assignments had been made, and the only thing to do at this point was to follow orders.

There was no way for me to know at the time what the mission would be like. An agent could never know that beforehand. And, in this case, that was probably a good thing. Because if I had known what the mission would be like, I very well might have walked into the hallway, taken the elevator to street level, hailed a taxi, and headed home to put my head under the covers.

3. THE PROFESSOR

When my neighborhood friends asked me about my new school, there were many things I couldn't tell them.

I couldn't tell them about Codes class.

I couldn't tell them about Counter-Espionage class.

I couldn't tell them about the Gadget Construction lab.

The only thing I *could* tell them about was my locker. Being assigned that private storage spot, protected by a combination lock, with vents at the top and the bottom, was the highlight of my first week at the Institute. I felt like a spy every time I opened it.

But telling my friends about my locker didn't impress them. It turned out that my locker was no different from their lockers. Apparently, there was no special locker designed for spies. In that respect, at least, the Institute was no different from any other middle school.

Lucy's locker was a different story. I wish I could have told my friends about *that*. It was like an origami museum. Every time she folded a new piece, she added it to the collection. By the time we were assigned that first mission, the landscape of her locker was filled with lions, swans, wizards, and Wookies. She even had a model of the White House in there.

As I approached her locker, still baffled and confused from my conversation with Poppleton, I could see she had added to the collection. A freshly-folded x-wing fighter made from a Subway wrapper was hanging from the ceiling of the locker as if patrolling the skies above the strangest planet ever.

"What took so long?" Lucy asked as she saw me approaching. "I thought maybe he had taken us off the mission or something."

"No, he was just ... " I paused for a moment. I wanted to tell her about the envelope, but I couldn't. Poppleton had told me to keep that to myself. "Uh ... he was just telling me to be extra careful is all."

She gave me a skeptical look. "Well, okay then, let's get down to Red Station. Lenny and Isabel are waiting for us."

I became more and more nervous as we walked down the three flights of stairs and through the long, narrow hallway that led to Red Station. A Level One mission would have made me nervous enough. The fact that the Syndicate was involved, and that Poppleton felt the need to warn me to be extra careful, made it worse. By the time we arrived, my breathing was shallow, my mouth was dry, and my stomach was fluttering like a flag in a strong breeze.

Lenny and Isabel were standing against the far wall of Red Station, in front of the East hatch, when we entered. They were preparing their mission packs while Red Station Chief mapped our course on his computer system.

"Decided to join us, huh?" Lenny said as he looked up from his pack. His voice conveyed the false authority of someone who thought he was more important than he actually was. "We are ready to go as soon as the chief gets our route figured out. Should be pretty simple. I think it is all Red Line for us today."

Red Station Chief gave Lenny an irritated glance from behind the command desk. He obviously could tell when an agent was acting self-important. He had been an agent himself once, and had spent years as a line mapper before he was promoted to station chief. They didn't give that job to just anyone. They needed someone who knew the network of tunnels, passages, and entry points under the city and who could guide agents safely to a final destination.

"Here we go," Red Station Chief said as he released the lock on the East hatch and swung the heavy metal door open. He checked each of our packs as we stepped through the hatch and into the long, narrow tunnel of the Red Line. A narrow cable hung from the ceiling of the tunnel, stretching out in front of us until it disappeared in the darkness.

I felt anticipation swell in my chest. The Red Line was legendary among agents. Our Underground History teacher told us that parts of it were more than 100 years old. It was built at the same time as the Institute. It was like a narrow hallway beneath the city that stretched for miles.

Of course, it was only a small part of the overall plan. The founders of the Institute were smart that way: they knew traveling underground would be an advantage for us. So every time a new subway line was bored through the ground, or the foundation for a skyscraper dug out, or maintenance tunnels for utility lines created, the founders sent workers from the Institute to create access points and add extra tunnels. Over time, they built an underground transportation system—with zip lines, secret tunnels, and access points that reached into subway lines and buildings throughout the city—that was every bit as complicated and powerful as anything above the ground.

"It's pretty straightforward," Red Station Chief said as we attached our zip handles to the cable. "You'll just take the line to location 1547. Should take about fifteen minutes. Once you're there, the hatch on the Northwest side of the tunnel will drop you right into a supply closet. Open that door and you'll be inside the University subway station. The rest is above ground. I've transmitted everything to your spy specs."

Spy specs. That was another reason I was excited. This would be my first chance to use spy specs out in the field. We had used them a bunch of times in training, but I had never worn them outside of the Institute.

Officially we were supposed to call them F.F.V.A.S.A.R. devices. It was short for Franklin's Fantastic Visual Aid for Secret Agents of the Revolution. That was the name Ben Franklin gave them. Yes, *the* Ben Franklin. He was the very first Gadgets teacher at the Institute. He came up with some great ideas, but he wasn't modest, and he definitely wasn't concise. He clearly never thought about trying to yell out, "Hey, put on your F.F.V.A.S.A.R. devices," in the middle of a chase. Too many letters. So we called them spy specs instead.

Anyway, the beauty of spy specs was that they looked just like ordinary eyeglasses from the outside. But from the inside, they let us see and do all sorts of things. Starting with the built-in navigation screen that showed an entire map of the underground city, like a complex spider web, with our route highlighted in red.

"Oh, and one more thing," Red Station Chief said as our zip handles began to hum and propel us away from him. "You'll want to activate the night vision on your spy specs. Watch for the sagging sewer line under 14th avenue."

It was hard to see much of anything as we reached full speed. Most of the tunnel was a blur. Still, it was exciting to be on my first trip through one of the tunnels with a zip line.

I almost began to forget I was nervous.

Almost, but not quite.

Everything went according to plan. At location 1547, we entered a supply closet through a hatch door set in the cement wall. From there, it was just a matter of sneaking into the subway station, joining the crowd as it walked up the stairs to the street, walking the two blocks to the science building, and entering the conference room through the lobby entrance.

That was when things got interesting.

The conference room was filled with people. They stood around in small groups, talking and laughing and just generally doing nothing.

It was exactly the sort of situation they had trained us for at the Institute. We were supposed to try to blend in. That, after all, was one big advantage of using kids as agents. They could go places and do things that adult spies couldn't. Adults saw them, but they didn't really notice them. They ignored them, or talked to them like they were four-year-olds, or even asked them what their favorite classes were in school. But what most adults never did was suspect kids of spying.

Once we had entered the room, Lenny didn't hesitate. He waded through the crowd, completely at ease. He chatted with people as if he belonged. Of course, he didn't. But nobody could tell from the way he was acting.

Lenny's method for blending in was the same one they taught in all the textbooks. Act like you belonged by being outgoing, sociable, the life of the party. In short, by acting like everybody else. It worked well for him because he could pull it off. He was a natural at it.

I tried this method once in class. Let's just say I wasn't a natural at it. It wasn't my style. Not even close.

You see, I wasn't a fan of crowds. Put me in a room with more than a few other people, and I started to feel like Marlin being chased by Bruce the shark.

So I developed my own method.

I liked to think that some day it would be taught in the textbooks also. I called it "the Nate method" of blending in. It was simple, really: I blended in by pretending to be a very shy and self-conscious kid who didn't like crowds.

I was very good at it. That was probably because it didn't require me to act. It was easy for me to look shy and self-conscious because I *was* shy and self-conscious. For me, it came down to just looking like myself.

I figured it worked because no one ever *wanted* to look shy and insecure. So if you saw a kid looking all shy, like he was hiding from the crowd, you wouldn't suspect him. You would feel sorry for him. That was what my method counted on. Sympathy.

Lucy, of course, was good at either method. She could blend in by acting popular, or she could blend in by looking shy. Honestly, she could blend in just about anywhere. Lucy was what we in the spy trade called a versatile blender.

Usually, though, Lucy preferred to hang out with me. So we stood in the corner, trying to look as uncomfortable as we could while Lenny and Isabel worked the room.

We had been there only five minutes when Professor Wilson approached us. Honestly, Lucy and I were a bit startled. Lenny and Isabel were supposed to be the ones to make contact with the subject. Not us. We were just sixth graders. We were there to watch and to learn.

The fact that he came straight to us should have been my first indication that something was wrong. No experienced agent—let alone a friend of Poppleton's—would mistake Lucy or me for a seventh or eighth grader.

Why, then, had Professor Wilson come straight to us rather than seek out our mission leader? It was a crucial question, but I didn't have time to think much about it.

I was too struck by Professor Wilson's appearance. He was worse at blending in than I was. He was a large and rather plump man with white hair and a white beard. His face was flushed red, as if he had just run a marathon. There was a thin film of sweat across his brow.

His eyes shifted from side to side while he craned his neck to look first over one shoulder, then over the other. He looked like a Santa Claus who had run out of presents and was being chased by a mob of angry children.

"Poppleton sent you, I assume?" He spoke in a hushed tone but with a sense of urgency. He looked nervous and scared and barely made eye contact as he spoke to us.

We both nodded as Lucy gave a businesslike reply. "Affirmative."

"We don't have much time. You were followed," he said as his eyes continued to scan the room. "I spotted a Syndicate agent in the hallway."

"I don't see how," I said. The very thought seemed ridiculous. "We came straight from the Institute. You know, through the tunnels. How could anyone have followed us?"

Professor Wilson looked stunned. "Straight from the Institute? Below ground?"

Lucy and I both nodded.

"It's worse than I thought, then. We don't have much time." He paused and leaned in closer as he took one more look over his shoulder. "It isn't safe here. You need to … "

His voice trailed off as he looked over his shoulder at a group of three adults standing behind him. They appeared to be having a conversation but easily could have been eavesdropping on our conversation while pretending to chat. After all, spies pretended all the time. I, for example, was pretending to be shy and uncomfortable at that exact moment.

"Yes. Yes, indeed. Interesting point," said Professor Wilson in a loud and booming voice that caught me off guard. It took me a second to realize that he was pretending, too. I was about to respond when he thrust a small piece of paper into my hand. "Here's my business card. Make sure you share that with your teacher. I bet your results will be interesting."

"Okay, thanks," I said. "Um, anything else you'd suggest?"

"Oh, yes, you mentioned you would like a picture taken with me. Let's do that right now." He motioned me toward the wall.

It was a clever tactic, designed to create distance between us and anybody who might be eavesdropping. They taught us that in an evasive maneuvers unit at the Institute. It worked every time.

"Y-y-yes a photo would be great," I said in a more hesitant tone than I intended.

Lucy caught on right away, pulling a cell phone from her pocket. The tactic worked. The adults that seemed to be eavesdropping were frozen in place, unable to move closer without interfering with Lucy, who remained standing where we had been.

As Lucy pretended to be confused over which button to press, how to focus, and how to make sure we were both smiling, Professor Wilson whispered gently so that only I could hear him.

"You must be very careful. The agent I saw is named Ivan." He paused as Lucy told us to move a little closer together, then over to the left. "He was a student at the Institute years ago, before he turned and started working for the Syndicate. Very smart. Very well-trained. And, unfortunately, ruthless. He will try to stop you from completing your mission at all costs. Just watch for him please. You'll recognize him because of the scar. It's on his face. You can't miss it."

"Oh, I don't think we need to worry," I said quickly. "We are going straight back to the Institute. And, anyway, we have Lenny and Isabel along to protect us."

Professor Wilson stared at me with a mixture of surprise and disbelief. It was the sort of look you might give someone standing on the edge of a cliff during a windstorm, but who insisted everything was safe. "You really don't understand, do you?"

"Well, I thought I did, but—" I paused as he leaned closer.

"Look, think about it. How did the Syndicate know you would be here? Nobody else knew I was coming here to meet you, so how did they know?"

I suddenly realized what he was getting at. If the Syndicate didn't follow us, then the only way they could have known we would be here was if someone at the Institute had told them. Someone at the Institute, one of our fellow agents, had betrayed us.

I shook my head, not wanting to believe the only logical conclusion. "No, that can't be."

"But it's the only explanation, don't you see? There is a traitor in your midst. You must take it seriously."

"Smile," Lucy said as her cell phone clicked.

"Very good. I must get going," Professor Wilson said, clearly anxious to leave. His eyes locked on mine for a moment as he continued, "You go ahead and pair that picture up with that card I gave you and you should be all set."

Professor Wilson turned on his heels, glanced at the group of adults standing behind him, and then moved quickly toward the door. His gait was stiff but hurried, like he wasn't used to walking fast but felt like he had to get away urgently.

He was right to worry.

As I stuffed the business card in my pocket, I noticed the group of adults follow him out of the room. They didn't look stiff at all. They moved with the gracefulness of athletes. Or, just maybe, spies. It didn't look to me like he had much chance of outrunning them, if that was his plan.

Here was the surprising thing: not one of them stayed behind. It made no sense. We had been seen talking to Professor Wilson. He had even handed me a piece of paper. Most agents would have found that suspicious and followed the two of us. But not a single one of them did that.

I didn't ask myself why they didn't leave an agent behind to watch us.

I didn't ask myself why all three of them pursued Professor Wilson.

I didn't ask myself why they didn't glance in our direction as they left.

I didn't ask myself—I didn't even *think* to ask myself—any of those things. I was either too shocked by the thought of a double agent, or too confused by Professor Wilson's last words to us, "pair that picture up with that card I gave you and you should be all set."

But it didn't matter. I would discover the answers to all those questions soon enough.

And when I did, I would realize that our situation was more precarious than I had feared.

4. THE ENEMY AGENT

"Nate, we need to get moving." Lucy grabbed my arm and pulled me toward the door.

"But what about the information? Professor Wilson didn't give us the information we came for."

"It doesn't matter," Lucy said. "We'll figure it out when we get back. We can't stay here. Quick, give Lenny and Isabel the signal."

I hesitated for a moment. I knew exactly what Lucy meant, of course. Agents at the Institute used signals to communicate without talking. It was a skill that was taught in Signals class every Tuesday and Thursday. We learned every sort of signal you could imagine. Eye signals, hand signals, leg signals, and even ear signals (yes, I could signal with my ears). I could even order my lunch in the cafeteria using nothing but nostril flares. That one was for extra credit.

The problem was that this situation required a very complicated set of signals. *Hey, we made contact with Professor Wilson and he gave me his card, and now some people are chasing him and we need to get back to the Institute*—it was a mouthful to say, let alone signal. It would take all the arm, ear, and nose coordination I could muster.

Lenny was on the other side of the room. As Lucy and I headed for the door, I let out a breath and prepared to deliver a symphony of signals that would dazzle my fellow agents. This moment, I knew, was my opportunity to become a signaling legend. I imagined the possibilities if I pulled it off: I could see myself at a school assembly, being presented the monthly trophy for Astute Signaling under Pressure, with all the students in the school cheering.

There was just one problem. I forgot the signal.

Signaling under pressure, no matter how much I studied, wasn't my strong suit. Give me some history, an equation, or even some poetry and I could keep it sealed in my brain like a peanut butter and jelly sandwich in a ziplock bag. But give me a signal, ask me to remember it under pressure, and I was clueless. I was what the agents at the Institute called a "classroom signaler." That just meant I could remember signals in class (when I didn't need them) but not under pressure (when I did).

I had the same problem when I tried playing baseball. The coach was always giving these signals—wiping his face, scratching his head, slapping his shoulder—but I couldn't tell if he was giving a signal or just had fleas. That was why baseball never worked out for me. Well, that, and the fact that I couldn't throw. Those two things pretty much ended my baseball career at an early age.

Uncertain of the proper signal, I did what any spy would do in that situation: I improvised. I looked straight into Lenny's eyes, patted my chest frantically with one hand and pointed to the doorway with the other. It was pretty much the universal signal for, *I am going over there*. Obviously, it wasn't one that they taught us in Signals class.

Lenny, obviously unaccustomed to my straightforward signaling, looked baffled.

I hoped Isabel, standing in the other corner of the room, would catch on. Isabel, you see, was a master at signals. She was the one that, month after month, enjoyed the adulation of all the agents at the weekly assembly. In fact, at our school, there was a nickname for the Astute Signaling under Pressure Trophy: we called it the Isabel.

At that moment, though, Isabel didn't need signals to communicate what she was thinking. Her look said it all. Whatever the signal was for *What are you doing, you buffoon?* it couldn't have been nearly as effective as the cool, contemptuous stare she delivered.

It wasn't the first time I had received that look from an eighth grade girl. It happened to me all the time. Still, I was grateful that only an instant later Lucy pulled me through the doorway and into the relative privacy of the building lobby.

"Dude that was like the worst signaling I've ever seen," Lucy teased as she chuckled and rolled her eyes. "I don't even want to know what you would do if you wanted to signal that you needed to use the rest room."

I laughed and blushed. There was no point trying to act cool. "Yeah, I've done better. Let's get out of here. Lenny and Isabel can catch up with us in the subway station. I'm too embarrassed to hang around here."

As we turned to go outside, I felt the disappointment of a mission only half-accomplished. We didn't get the information we came for. Our contact seemed to be in danger. We were no closer to defeating the Syndicate. It wasn't exactly the sort of result most agents hoped for when they set out on a mission.

Even so, I tried to look on the positive side. At least we remained safe. We had time to figure out another plan, and I knew that once we returned to the Institute Poppleton would know what to do.

We had taken one step toward the outer doorway when we saw him.

Emerging from the shadows of the otherwise-empty lobby, perhaps thirty feet from where we were standing, was an average-sized man with average height, average weight, average-length arms, and probably even an average waist size. Even his wrists and ankles appeared to be average. Everything about his size screamed, *I'm average. Don't notice me!*

In fact, I may not have looked at him twice if not for the fact that everything he was wearing was blue. Blue shoes, blue socks, blue pants, blue belt, blue sweater, and blue stocking hat. Even his watch was blue. Then there were those gloves. Yep, you guessed it: they were blue.

It was as if he shopped at a store that sold only blue. The Blue Depot. Blues-R-Us. The Blues Authority. Something like that.

His eyes were separated by the narrowest, pointiest nose I had ever seen. A thick, straight strip of licorice-black eyebrow sat beneath a rectangular forehead that disappeared into his blue stocking hat. His teeth were bright white, like headlights inside the dim light of the building lobby.

They were striking features. Spy-like, really.

But I didn't spend more than a second noticing his clothing, his gloves, his watch, or his eyebrows. I focused on something else, something that made me freeze in place as motionless as a freshly-rolled snowman: there, on his left cheek, was a thin scar stretching from his ear down to his chin.

I realized with a jolt that this was the agent Professor Wilson had warned me about. Ivan, he had called him. To me, he looked more like Agent Blue. Sorry, but what else should I have called someone who dressed like they owned stock in a company that made blue dye?

Now it was clear why none of the three agents inside had stayed to follow us: they didn't need to. They had Agent Blue for that.

Normally I would have spent some time processing this information. At that moment, though, I didn't have time to process much of anything. Agent Blue wasn't just standing there. He was coming toward us.

He moved with the confidence and agility of an experienced agent. It was easy to see. Agents were like athletes that way: you could usually recognize the good ones right away. They were soft on their feet. Graceful, even. But it was always clear that with a moment's notice, they could transform into swift and deadly spying machines.

"Hey there, I need to talk to you two," Agent Blue said with a menacing grin. He needed to work on his grinning skills. A grin—even a spy grin—was supposed put people at ease. His grin did the opposite: it made the hair on my arms shiver. I'm pretty sure that if this had been an episode of *Star Wars*, the Darth Vader music would have been playing in the background about then.

We didn't wait around to see what he was grinning about. By then it could have been too late. We turned and began walking quickly in the opposite direction, down the long hallway that led away from the exit doors.

"He's cutting off our route back to the subway station," Lucy said as Agent Blue pursued us down the hallway. "We'll need to find another way back to school."

"There's probably an access point somewhere in this building," I said as we neared the end of the hallway. "Let's get to a safe spot where we can do a search."

"Quick, this way," Lucy said as she pulled me through a doorway to the basement stairwell. We took the stairs two at a time and were two floors down before we heard the door open and Agent Blue racing down the stairs in pursuit.

Two more floors down at full speed and we were in the dark basement hallway. Dusty old chairs, desks, and bookshelves lined the walls. It felt like a graveyard for office furniture. We weaved among tables and lecterns as we raced down the hallway, searching desperately for a good hiding place.

All we needed, we both knew, was a simple out-of-the-way place where no one would think to look for us. Once we found it, we could simply wait as Agent Blue continued searching. That would give Lenny and Isabel time to come to our rescue. Or, if they didn't, we could wait until the danger had passed, then make our way back to the Institute.

But there were no hiding places. Among the desks and chairs scattered through the basement, there was nothing even remotely suitable as a hiding place for two agents.

We reached the end of the hallway at the same time as Agent Blue started down the last flight of stairs. We could hear his footsteps as they came closer and closer. In only seconds, he would be at the other end of the hallway. We would be in full view, trapped at the end of a basement hallway.

That was when I saw it: leaning against the wall, directly beneath a small square opening in the tile ceiling, was a simple stepladder. It took us only seconds to climb the ladder and work our way through the opening. I reached down and pulled the ladder up behind us just as Agent Blue entered the other end of the hallway.

Then we waited.

Agent Blue worked his way methodically down the hallway, checking every room and turning over every piece of furniture. Gradually, he reached the end of the hallway, and he had no more rooms to check. He stood there, directly below us, separated from our view by thin ceiling tiles. The hallway was quiet except for his raspy breathing.

It seemed as if he stood there, motionless, forever. I counted at least 200 beats of my heart which, given how nervous I felt, might have happened in only a few seconds.

Suddenly, we heard a loud beep. Then his voice echoed in the hallway. "Yeah, it's Ivan. I followed them into the basement, but they must've found a way out. I'm coming back up. They must be on the street. Monitor all frequencies."

We stayed motionless as he walked up the hallway and climbed the stairs, the sound of his footsteps growing fainter with every step until, eventually, he was gone.

"Man, that was close," said Lucy. "Let's get back to The Institute before he decides to come back."

"I'll check the route."

All the work Red Station Chief had put into mapping our route was useless now. We needed to find another way back to The Institute.

Luckily, we could use our spy specs for that.

You see, one of the great things about our spy specs was the Tunnel Locater. We called it the TL, and it did exactly what it sounded like: showed us all the tunnels, access points, and crawlspaces we could use to travel through buildings and underground. It was basically a mobile version of the mapping system the station chiefs used to map routes for agents when they started their missions. It wasn't as good as a plan designed by an experienced station chief, but for agents in our situation it was the next best thing.

I watched the right lens of my spy specs as the TL slowly focused on our position, narrowing the view from a city-wide map to a map of our current location. I could see why other agents always said the TL was our most valuable tool. Without it, Lucy and I would be stuck in the basement of a building with no chance of escape.

Knowing the tunnels came in handy.

In this case, for example, Agent Blue was thinking about hallways and doorways, floors and ceilings, streets and cars. But we were thinking about tunnels and access points and utility ducts. We saw a world that he didn't see.

"There is an access point about ten feet ahead on the right," I said.

"Man, they could use a vacuum cleaner in this place," Lucy said as she crawled across the dusty ceiling tiles.

"There it is." I pointed toward what looked like a cupboard door attached to the outer wall. "Looks like that crawl space connects to some sort of ventilation that leads right to the subway tunnel. It will drop us right on top of the subway car. We can get to the station from there."

"Perfect." Lucy wasted no time. She was on her hands and knees with the door open in seconds.

I followed quickly, and we both crawled furiously through dust and cobwebs of the crawlspace before entering the narrow ventilation shaft that would lead us to the subway tunnel.

Crawling through the tunnels was nothing like what I had imagined. I had imagined feeling excited and important, like a super smart, super tough, super spy-like spy. But instead I felt dirty, scared, and tired. I didn't feel spy-like at all. I felt more like a pet hamster.

"Which way?" Lucy asked as we reached a point where the shaft split into two directions, one to the left and one to the right.

I checked the TL. "Take a left, and then get ready for a slide."

Sure enough, a few more feet of crawling and the gently sloping floor of the shaft became steeper and steeper until, without much warning, it became so steep that we could no longer crawl but began to slide uncontrollably.

"Get ready," I said as my TL began to flash furiously and I could see the tunnel entrance (or, in our case, the exit) ahead of us. Seconds later, we fell from the opening and landed feet first on the roof of a New York City Subway car.

I don't know if you have ever stood on the top of a New York City Subway car. I hope not, because it is no place for kids (or adults for that matter). But let me tell you something: my first thought when I collected myself wasn't that the roof was dirty (it was), or that air smelled clean and fresh (it didn't), or that Lucy's face looked like she was wearing a beard of cobwebs (it did). No, my first thought was this: *must get down.*

You see, there was nothing fun about being on the roof of a train. For one thing, we were high off the ground. For another thing, I knew that the train could start moving any second. After all, that was what subway trains did: they moved. Sometimes they moved very fast, and I didn't want to be on top of that train when it started moving.

So I didn't spend time enjoying the scenery or chatting with Lucy.

I looked for a way down.

The car we stood on was maybe a dozen cars from the end of the train. All we needed to do was hop from car to car until we reached the last one. Then we could climb down, find an access point to the Red Line, and return to the Institute.

I began to relax as the path to safety became clear. Very soon, I expected, we would be back at the Institute, filling Poppleton in on the details of our mission as he set out to create another plan for dealing with the threat from the Syndicate. I expected that, now that he knew the nature of the threat and the fact that there was a double agent in our midst, he would assign our very best agents to the next mission.

Needless to say, that would mean Lucy and I would get a chance to recover behind the safe walls of the Institute. Perhaps I would get a chance to crack a few codes, or finish my assignment in Codes class. Either way, I would be safe.

The relaxed feeling stayed with me as we walked the length of the first car and hopped onto the roof of the next one. It didn't last long. Before I had fully recovered my breath, I heard a loud crash, like someone banging against the lid of a garbage can, echo throughout the tunnel.

Lucy grasped my arm and gasped. "Nate, look!"

I was already looking. And what I saw made my heart sink.

It was Agent Blue.

Normally, I might have tried to figure out how he had known where to find us. After all, when he left the hallway he had been headed upstairs to street level. To end up where we were, he would have had to turn around and come back down the stairs. But I didn't have time to think about those things because at that moment, he was sprinting toward us.

5. THE SUBWAY

The engineers and builders who designed the New York City Subway spent a lot of time thinking before they started building.

They thought about sewer lines and electrical cables.

They thought about digging trenches and planting explosives.

They thought about support beams, concrete walls, and ventilation.

They even thought about long maintenance shafts stretching from tunnels to streets, like enormous straws connecting the underground city to the above-ground city.

What they didn't think about was head room. They didn't plan for people to be walking on top of the subway train, and they certainly didn't plan for a couple of kids like us to be chased by Agent Blue.

I could see the problem as soon as Lucy and I turned to run. We had dropped into a part of the tunnel where the gap between the subway train and the ceiling was large enough for us to stand. Even Agent Blue, taller than us by a foot, had enough headroom to break into a sprint without any concerns about bumping his head against the steel beams on the tunnel ceiling. But several cars in front of us the gap narrowed to only a few feet.

Once we reached that point we wouldn't be able to run. We would need to drop to our bellies and crawl.

I had nothing against crawling. I could do the alligator crawl with the best of them. But I was also smart enough to know that no one ever crawled their way to safety. No, escaping from someone like Agent Blue required something different, something either faster or more creative.

Agent Blue didn't seem worried about the ceiling. That was probably because, even though Lucy and I were running at our top speed, he was closing the distance between us. I had never seen anyone run so fast. At this rate, we wouldn't even make it to the area with the low ceiling before he caught us.

"Nate, I don't think we're going to be able to outrun him," Lucy panted as she looked over her shoulder.

He was only a few strides behind us now, gliding effortlessly across the roof of the subway train. He didn't seem tired or concerned. No, he seemed energetic and confident, as if he expected to complete his mission in the next few seconds. And I could tell from the look in his steely gaze that Agent Blue wasn't the type to let kids like us stand between him and a completed mission.

Just as I was beginning to think that we had no hope of escaping, I saw something that gave me a jolt of excitement. Perhaps twenty steps ahead of us, just beyond the point where the tunnel narrowed, a dim circle of light the size of a hula-hoop shone on the roof of the subway car.

It was the light from a maintenance shaft. Maintenance shafts were built in almost every tunnel in the subway to connect the subway tunnel to the street above. If this shaft were like all the others, it would have a locked grate at the top and bottom entrances.

A maintenance shaft was the perfect solution. If we could get it open and get inside before Agent Blue captured us, we wouldn't have to outrun him at all. We could just lock him on the other side, climb the shaft to the street, and get back to The Institute above ground.

"Lucy, a maintenance shaft," I shouted as I pointed to the circle of light. "You stall him. I'll get it open."

The builders of the subway may not have planned for this sort of situation, but the builders at The Institute *did*. They made sure that we had a master key that would fit every lock in the subway system.

Lucy nodded. I could tell she was thinking the same thing I was. With Agent Blue only steps behind us, this was our only chance. "Okay, you get inside and give me the signal when you are ready. I won't have much time."

"Shouldn't take me long. Try to buy me half a minute." I reached into my mission pack for the master key as I spoke.

You might think it odd that I would let a girl fight my battles for me. It wasn't the way things usually happened in the movies, after all. Well, Lucy was tough. Way tougher than me. Every day in Battle Training class, Lucy dominated the other agents, even seventh and eighth graders. She did windmill kicks, hand chops, and fancy little spinning somersaults in the air that ended with devastating gut punches. Yes, indeed, if you ever find yourself in a subway tunnel facing an opponent like Lucy, I suggest you run.

I would like to tell you that I dominated Spy Battle class also but, well, let's just say that Mr. Mulligan felt my time would be better spent *observing* rather than, you know, actually *participating* in battle training. I suppose that was because of the accident. On the first day of school, walking down the stairs, I tripped over my shoelaces, reached out my arms for balance, and basically shoved Mr. Mulligan down a flight of stairs.

I was fine. He ended up with a cast on one arm. Ever since, I have been a battle *observer* rather that a battle *participant*.

I rushed toward the maintenance shaft as Lucy turned to face Agent Blue. For the first time, I saw a shocked look on his face. It was as if no one had ever decided to turn and fight him before. Or perhaps he expected the boy to be the one who turned to fight. Whatever the reason for it, the surprise made him pause when he came to a stop in front of Lucy.

"Look, all I want is the chip," he said in his gravelly voice. "Just give it to me and this will be over."

It made no sense. I had no idea what he was talking about.

Lucy seemed as baffled as I was.

What chip? A potato chip? If that was what he wanted, I could point him to about a dozen grocery stores within just a few blocks. Really, for a potato chip, this was a lot of trouble to go through.

But I suspected he was after something more important than a potato chip.

By time, I was lying on my back beneath the entrance to the maintenance shaft. It took me only a second to find the rusty lock and insert the key. As I tried to turn it, though, it became stuck. The lock clearly hadn't been used for years. I jiggled and jiggled the key, trying to work the lock free, turning to check on Lucy as I struggled.

Agent Blue had recovered from his shock and showed no more hesitation. He ran right at her, aiming an expertly-timed kick right at her chest. It was a powerful kick, and if it had landed Lucy would have been sent flying.

But Lucy was ready. She ducked under the kick, and as his kicking leg sailed over her head she landed two quick hand chops to his lower back and a sharp kick to the leg he stood on. It was enough to force his leg to collapse, leaving him literally without a leg to stand on.

He landed against the top of the subway car like a boulder falling from a cliff as Lucy quickly backed away to a safe position.

If that had been me, I would have stayed where I was and admitted defeat, but he did no such thing.

He rose and turned and, before Lucy could react, he reached into his pocket and pulled out a small object the size of a golf ball, but perfectly round and shiny, and a shade of blue that perfectly matched his outfit.

His arm was like a blur as he threw the blue ball right at Lucy's chest. It landed with the force of a punch and sent her staggering backwards.

She steadied herself. Then, with a look in my direction, held her arms up as if to say, "What, not yet?"

The simple motion caused Agent Blue to pause and look at me. A creepy smile slowly replaced the tension on his face. The surprise of Lucy's challenge had faded. He was alert and steady as he reached into his pocket for another ball. And, I would soon find out, he was now fully aware of my plan.

I assumed he would throw the ball at Lucy.

From the look on her face, I was pretty sure that Lucy assumed he would throw it at her, too.

But he didn't throw it at Lucy.

He threw it at me.

It was the last thing I expected. After all, I was an observer, not a participant. Apparently Agent Blue didn't know that. Or maybe he just didn't care.

It took me a split second to realize what had happened. One moment I was jiggling the lock furiously and the next a rock-hard shiny blue ball was coming toward my face at 80 miles per hour.

I jerked my head to the side as the ball grazed my right earlobe. If I hadn't moved in time I would have been finished.

I will never know whether it was the adrenaline that did it or simply the fact that I had been jiggling the key in the lock for just the right amount of time, but just at that instant, even before I felt the sting on my earlobe, the lock came free with a loud click.

"Ten seconds," I yelled to Lucy as I tore open the metal grate that covered the opening to the maintenance shaft. I knew I was almost there. I could see the sky looking down at me through the long metal tube. There was a small metal ladder stretching to the top of the shaft, but I knew that I couldn't trust that. If the ladder were as old and rusty as the lock—and it looked like it was—then the rungs could have been weak from age and rust.

I didn't want to take that risk, not with Agent Blue in pursuit. Lucky for us, our full mission pack was equipped with a set of suction handles. They were the perfect fit for this situation. Made for climbing, they allowed us to attach to walls and climb, Spiderman-style, up buildings or walls or, for that matter, pretty much anything.

I attached the suction handle and pulled myself up into the shaft in one quick motion. The plan was working. The only part left was to give Lucy the signal. Once she joined me inside the shaft we would pull the grate shut behind us, and Agent Blue would be locked on the other side.

At least, that was what I thought to myself as I hung suspended from a suction handle inside a maintenance shaft that was built before my great-grandfather was born.

That was when something happened that I hadn't planned for.

The train lurched forward.

It shouldn't have been a surprise. After all, that was what trains usually did: they moved.

The problem, though, was that I hadn't even considered that this might happen. It forced me to make a decision. I could choose the safety of the shaft, but that would mean abandoning Lucy. Or, I could drop to the roof of the train, which would mean abandoning safety.

It took me only a split-second to decide. I couldn't abandon Lucy. So I disconnected the suction handle and dropped to the roof of the moving train with a thud.

Lucy and Agent Blue were engaged in a fierce battle just ten steps in front of me as I struggled to my feet atop the last subway car. Lucy attacked with a combination of windmill kicks and quick hand chops to the belly. She was in her comfort zone now. I almost felt sorry for Agent Blue.

The train picked up speed as they exchanged blows. The slightest mistake could have spelled doom for either one of them.

That was when I thought of something: Agent Blue hadn't seen me fall to the roof of the train. As far as he was concerned, only he and Lucy were on the train. I knew I could use it to our advantage and buy Lucy just the time she needed.

"Hey, Blue!" I yelled in a voice that sounded more like a screech. Not very creative, I know. I would have liked to yell a threat of some sort, or perhaps a sharply-worded criticism of the color blue. Even a blue-themed knock-knock joke would have been nice. But I kept it simple. And it worked.

Startled, Agent Blue twisted his head to look over his shoulder at me.

It was just the opportunity Lucy needed. I had seen her prepare to launch this attack many times in practice. It started from a simple two-legged stance, involved one stride, a jump into the air, and a somersault and spin ending with a devastating two-legged kick into the chest of her opponent. I had never seen it fail.

But, then, I had never seen her try it on top of a moving train. That was a factor she should have considered. The moment after she left the ground, just as she was in mid-somersault and preparing to uncoil the power of her somersault-spin kick, the train lurched violently to the left as it encountered a left turn in the track.

It surprised all three of us.

Agent Blue was flung backwards, rolling across the roof of the train until, at the last possible moment, he reached out and grabbed a roof vent with his gloved hand.

I thought I was history as I fell to the roof and slid toward the side of the subway car. At the last second, just as I was about to plunge over the side, I remembered that I had a suction handle in my hand. I managed to attach it just as my body began to slide over the side of the car.

But I wasn't about to complain. Lucy had it worse. As she flew through the air, the train turned beneath her. Left without solid footing she skipped off the roof like a flat pebble across a still pond, bouncing again and again and again across the roof until, finally, the last bounce sent her flying directly over the top of me.

She managed to give me a hard poke in the ribs with her elbow as she sailed past.

Hey, that's my job, I thought to myself.

I was sure she was doomed, and that she would be crushed under the moving car. But at the very last second, she reached out with both hands and grabbed my leg, holding on like her life depended on it. Which was good because, of course, it did.

In her situation, I would have been panicked. One slip and she would be pulled under the subway car and crushed. But she didn't seem the least bit scared.

That was just like Lucy. Nothing seemed to frighten her. At least, not that I could ever tell.

I was a different story. I was scared all the time. My mom always told me it didn't matter, that it wasn't whether or not you were scared but what you did when you were scared. Well, at that moment I had no idea what to do, but what I felt like doing was closing my eyes and hoping someone would rescue me.

Agent Blue had recovered and was inching his way over to us from a distance of less than ten feet. Ever so slowly he inched along the roof, with his hands splayed out flat against the shiny metal roof.

The first thing I noticed was his gloves. They seemed to be more than just run-of-the-mill, keep my hands warm when it's cold outside kind of gloves. They seemed to be made of some special kind of fabric, and they gripped the top of the subway car the way a spider gripped a wall.

The most important thing about those gloves at that moment, though, was that they were getting closer to me. Dangerously close. So close that it felt like in just a few more seconds, he would be able to grasp my hands. Or worse, pry them loose.

As I struggled to maintain my grip, I came up with a few tips for those who find themselves hanging from the side of a subway car being chased by an agent dressed in blue.

Tip #1 was easy: don't sneeze. That one was sort of obvious. Sneezing was never a good idea in pressure-packed, holding-on-to-a-moving-subway-car situations.

Tip #2 took a little more planning. In fact, it took the sort of planning I wished I had done that morning when I got out of bed. But you can learn from my mistakes. Here's the tip: if you think there is even the slightest chance that you'll need to hang onto or grip or grasp pretty much anything, do not, under any circumstances apply lotion to your hands in the morning.

Don't get me wrong. I liked lotion as much as anyone. It kept the hands nice and soft. But it was also slippery. It made holding onto a moving subway train a little bit like holding onto a wet bar of soap. And on that day, in that situation, being chased by Agent Blue, the last thing I needed was slippery hands.

He was now only inches from me. As he reached out, I could see he was preparing to pry my hands loose from the handle. I squirmed and tried to secure my grip, but it was no use.

He pried my left hand off of the handle, leaving me dangling from only my right hand, with Lucy still swinging from my legs.

"Look, this is simple," he said. "Just give me the chip and I will help you up."

He held out his hand as if to help me.

Again with the chip, I thought. *What was this guy talking about? And didn't he realize that, you know, if I had his precious chip I probably would have given it to him by now? What did I need a chip for? I wasn't even hungry.*

I tried to slide my hand as far away from him as possible. It wasn't easy. Did I mention the lotion? Slippery hands? Subway car moving at high speed? You get the picture. I squirmed and inched my grip to the very end of the handle. Then I ran out of space.

"Nate, look up." Lucy's voice sounded like she was yelling from inside a vacuum cleaner. "The tunnel."

My throat tightened as I looked up and saw what she meant. Only a few car lengths ahead, the subway tunnel narrowed drastically on our side. There were only inches separating the side of the train car from the concrete wall. There wasn't enough space for Lucy and me to fit through.

If we didn't do something quick, we would be crushed.

"Got it," I yelled. "Follow my lead."

In most stories I have read, this was the point where the main character usually revealed that he had trained for this situation his entire life. Maybe he admitted that he was secretly a ninja. Then, with almost no effort, unleashed some sort of acrobatic ninja move to escape danger.

That is exactly what I wished I could have admitted about myself.

There was just one problem: I hadn't been training for that situation my entire life. In fact, I hadn't trained for that situation at all. Not ever. I was what you might call a beginner at hanging from the side of a moving subway car when being chased by Agent Blue. And, honestly, no one who saw me try to put on socks while standing up ever mistook me for a ninja.

I considered using a Jedi mind trick to distract him. You know, "these aren't the kids you are looking for" with a slow and deliberate wave of the hand in front of his face. But I quickly realized this wasn't a practical solution. For one thing, I wasn't sure I had what you might call "real" Jedi powers. I had only ever used them on Charlie, after all. For another thing, with the speed of the train, and Lucy hanging off my foot, I didn't exactly have a hand to spare at that moment. Not unless I wanted to fall under the subway train and be crushed.

So there I was, hanging from the subway car, barely able to hold on (did I mention the lotion?), with Lucy hanging from my ankles, the tunnel narrowing, Agent Blue inches from prying my hand loose and sending us to our doom, and me without a single ninja move or Jedi mind trick to unleash.

Without any other options, I did what anyone in my position would have done: I took a shallow half-breath, gave Lucy a half-nod, and I let go.

6. THE OLD TUNNEL

One of the first things they taught us at the Institute was how to write a mission summary. Part of being an organized spy was being able to outline all the important things that happened on a mission without getting too wrapped up in the details. It was like writing a book report, really. Except, instead of turning our mission summaries in to the teacher, we read them in front of the whole school.

If I had written a mission summary for our mission so far, it would have looked something like this:

PURPOSE: RECEIVE INFORMATION FROM PROFESSOR WILSON (A.K.A. "THE SUBJECT").

OPPOSITION: THE SYNDICATE; AGENT BLUE.

ROUTE: RED LINE TO UNIVERSITY STATION.

MAJOR EVENTS: MADE CONTACT WITH THE SUBJECT; HANDED A BUSINESS CARD BY THE SUBJECT; WARNED ABOUT DOUBLE AGENT; DETECTED AGENTS OF THE SYNDICATE FOLLOWING THE SUBJECT; ENCOUNTERED AGENT BLUE; FLED FROM AGENT BLUE; HUNG FROM MOVING SUBWAY TRAIN; TOOK A HALF-BREATH, GAVE A HALF-NOD, AND LET GO.

You were probably thinking something like this when you read that last part: *A half-breath? A half-nod? Didn't this guy ever finish what he started? Surely, this was a situation that called for a deep breath and a knowing nod. Both of them full, obviously.*

Well, let me tell you something: if you thought I had time for a deep breath and a full nod, then you have watched too many movies or read too many comic books.

Life moved too fast for deep breaths and knowing nods. At least, *my* life did.

Oh, you were thinking something else?

Like, for example, why I decided to let go of a moving subway train and risk falling to a grisly death beneath the metal wheels of a subway car?

There's a simple answer to that question: It was the only thing to do, really.

It might have seemed like a rookie mistake, something that only a beginner agent would have done. After all, falling from a height of ten feet was bad enough. Throw the whole train-moving-at-high-speed thing into the mix and it must have seemed downright idiotic.

But here's the thing: I knew something Agent Blue did not.

He knew, of course, that when a person let go of a moving train they started to fall. Fast. Very fast. So fast, in fact, that it would take only seconds to hit the ground. So it was no surprise to him that the instant I let go, I began falling. I could see the look of satisfaction in his eyes. For him, it must have felt like a victory. He looked proud. If there had been time, he probably would have stood up and done some sort of victory dance.

He also knew that the tunnel was beginning to narrow. To keep from getting crushed he had to stay motionless, tightly hugging the top of the subway car. That was exactly what he did as I continued to fall. He pressed his cheek firmly against the roof of the subway car and seemed determined to make himself skinny.

What Agent Blue didn't know, and what you probably didn't know either, was that I wasn't a fool. I might have looked like one, I might have talked like one, and I might even have acted like one sometimes. But in this case I wasn't at all foolish.

I had a plan.

As we fell, Lucy let go of my ankle with one of her hands, maintaining her grip with the other. I knew exactly what she was doing. When my head was only feet from the ground, her grip tightened around my ankle. Then, a split-second later, I felt like she was trying to pull my leg off.

I looked back toward Lucy and saw exactly what I expected. She was holding my leg with one hand and with the other hand had unleashed her tunnel-chute.

You probably didn't know about the tunnel-chute.

Neither did Agent Blue.

That was what I knew when I let go of the subway train: tucked inside every agent's mission pack was a small parachute designed for situations just like this. It was a pretty simple device, really. We designed it in Gadgets class. Just like a parachute, except small and built in a way that allowed one to jump from a moving subway car and float unharmed to the ground.

Lucy's tunnel-chute was red with LOL written in bright yellow paint. That was text-speak for Laugh Out Loud. It was one of those acronyms the kids who text message used all the time. Lucy didn't really like text-speak. OMG, IMO and all that drove her nuts. She liked whole words. Putting text-speak on her tunnel-chute was her way of making fun of it. I didn't think anyone got the joke except her, but she didn't seem to care.

Anyway, funny or not, the LOL tunnel-chute worked perfectly.

We sailed slowly to the ground as the subway car squeezed through the narrow passage ahead with Agent Blue flattened against the roof like a helpless refrigerator magnet.

Once we stood back on solid earth, Lucy quickly folded her tunnel-chute and stuffed it back into her coat pocket. She didn't fold it into any fancy shapes, though. Even Lucy knew that we didn't have time for origami.

"Let's go—we need to find an access point," panted Lucy as she fiddled with her TL. "There should be one around here somewhere."

I looked around in the dim light of the tunnel. I had never actually stood on the ground of a train tunnel before. It wasn't exactly the preferred way for us to travel. The narrow zip line tunnels, carved behind the walls of the larger subway tunnels, were a much better choice. Safer and, of course, more secretive.

But every once in a while an agent ended up in one of the larger tunnels due to an emergency. Sometimes it was because of a collapse or flood in the narrow tunnel. Other times it was because of an escape maneuver like the one Lucy and I had just executed.

Either way, the Institute's Emergency Directive was very clear on this point: if an agent found himself in a train tunnel he was to remain undetected, locate an access point as soon as possible, and return to the relative safety of a narrow tunnel.

Lucy walked slowly along the wall. She paused every few steps until, with no warning, her TL began to flash. She had found an access point.

She ran both hands over the smooth, cool concrete. From only a few feet away, nothing was visible in the wall. Every square foot of wall looked the same as any other. Just a wide expanse of concrete stretching out on either side of us.

Lucy suddenly stiffened as her hand rested on a patch of wall at knee level.

"Here it is," she said as she looked over her shoulder at me with relief in her eyes. "Can you help? The latch is probably stuck."

I nodded and stood next to her with both hands on the wall. "Okay, on three."

"One, two, three," we said in unison before pushing against the wall.

I pushed with such force that my feet began to slide backward across the dirty subway floor. But I steadied myself and continued. It was the only way we were going to get through. Sometimes the latches needed a lot of force, especially when they hadn't been used for a while. And it sure seemed like this one hadn't been used in a long time. It wasn't even budging.

"Keep pushing," Lucy said as she backed away from the wall. "I have an idea."

At first, her idea didn't seem all that great to me. After all, how was one of us backing away from the wall going to help get the hatch open? If the force from two of us pushing wasn't good enough, I didn't see how the force from only one of us pushing was going to be any better.

It was only when she took a deep breath and got into that familiar two-legged stance that I understood what she had in mind. She took one long stride, made a jump in the air, and performed her usual somersault and spin as she sailed toward the wall. At the last second, she unleashed a powerful two-legged kick directly into the wall.

The entire wall shook from the force of her blow. I didn't envy that wall. If walls could get bruises, I was pretty sure that wall would have ended up with bruises in the morning.

"That did it!" I said as I felt the wall give way. The force of Lucy's kick had loosened the latch and a small doorway in the wall, invisible just seconds ago, had opened in front of us.

Lucy was the first to crawl through. As soon as she was on the other side of the opening, she started coughing and waving her arms in front of her face. "Man, cobweb central." *Cough, Cough.*

It wasn't as bad for me as I crawled through the opening to join her. That was one benefit of letting someone else crawl into a cobweb-covered tunnel ahead of you: they cleared out some of the cobwebs.

We were crouched in a narrow tunnel, barely large enough for us to stand up, stretching out in either direction. Cobwebs clung to the ceiling and walls and covered the ground like cottony moss.

I pushed the hatch door closed, listening for the reassuring sound of the latch clicking into place. We were safe, at least for the moment. Even if Agent Blue managed to get off that moving subway train, he wouldn't be able to find us now. There was no way someone was going to find that doorway from the other side.

"Nate, put your hand here," Lucy said as she guided my hand to a spot on the cool, clay-like soil of the tunnel floor. "It's a mark."

I ran my hand across the ground as if petting a cat. There was definitely something carved into the smooth tunnel floor. It took me only moments to trace the outlines with my fingers. It was a simple triangle.

"What's it for?" I asked.

"Oh, you missed class that day!" Lucy said. "We learned about these last week."

She was right. I had missed half a day of school last week. Even secret agents needed to go to the dentist every once in a while.

"So what is it?" I asked.

"It was that day that I folded Helm's Deep out of the newspaper. I even put the little—"

"Lucy," I said, cutting her off. "The mark. We were talking about the mark."

"Oh, yeah. Sorry." She paused for a moment. "Anyway, yes, the mark. They put marks like this next to every access point back when they made them. It's crazy to think about. They had people walking the subway tunnels at night putting these access points in."

"But why did they mark them?" I asked.

"Well, back then agents were walking these tunnels with lanterns. These marks used to have some sort of powder in them that reflected light. It made it easier to see where the hatches were."

It made sense. With no TL and only the dim light of a lantern, it would have been hard to see anything against the walls of this tunnel. But I was thinking something else. "Well, all I know is that I'm sure glad someone thought to put these tunnels and access points in here."

"No kidding," Lucy said as she stood and waved her arms around to clear a space for us to stand. "Activate night vision."

She could have saved her breath. Mine was already activated. The only thing I hated more than tunnels were dark tunnels. I never needed to be told to activate night vision.

One thing was clear as I stood and surveyed the tunnel: no one had passed through this tunnel in years, perhaps even decades. No, this tunnel looked like it was from another century altogether. It was nothing like the narrow tunnels we usually used, with their smooth walls, metal beams, and suspended zip lines. This one had rough walls that showed the markings of shovels and pick-axes, sagging wooden beams, and not even the hint of a zip line.

We had studied these tunnels in Underground History class. They were from the earliest days of underground travel, built when The Institute first moved to its current location. In those days, agents actually walked through these tunnels, sometimes taking days to complete missions.

The old tunnels were abandoned years ago, replaced by newer tunnels that were bored through the earth with machines. But every so often we heard stories of agents using the old tunnels as shortcuts, or for emergencies, or even just because they were curious.

Lucy was fiddling with her spy specs, probably searching for a route on the Tunnel Locater. "We need to get back to school. I'd really like to know why that guy was chasing us."

"I know. And what chip was he talking about, anyway? Maybe Poppleton can help us figure it out. We can't stay here," I said.

"This way." Lucy gave the signal that she had located our position.

According to the TL, we were in an old, abandoned section of narrow tunnel that intersected the Red Line just ahead. We worked our way down the tunnel, walking single-file to squeeze through the narrow sections, and waving away cobwebs with every step. It was like walking on a cloud, our feet invisible in the thick, fluffy whiteness of the cobwebs on the floor.

As we got closer to the intersection, I was sure I could hear the soft whir of zip handles moving along the Red Line. Other agents, I assumed, returning from their missions. Or, perhaps it was Lenny and Isabel returning from our mission.

I began to relax, knowing we were close to safety. As soon as we reached the Red Line we could attach to the zip line and get back to Red Station in only minutes. Then we would be safe within the walls of The Institute. There would be a debriefing session with Poppleton.

Then, a simple day of classes. No more chasing, riding the tops of subway trains, or crawling on the floors of old tunnels.

At least, that was what I thought as we walked through the cloud of cobwebs toward The Institute.

But just as we approached the intersection of the old tunnel and the Red Line, only minutes from the relative safety of Red Station and the Institute, I felt the vibration of a code red alert coming from my spy specs. Three quick bursts followed by a moment of silence. Then another three quick bursts followed by silence.

I grabbed Lucy's arm, knowing before I even saw the text in my right lens that this wouldn't be good news. I had never witnessed a code red, of course. No current agent had. The last one was more than twenty years ago. But we all knew what they were and what they meant. A code red meant the Institute was in grave danger.

There was a brief red flash on the lens of my spy specs as a short message from Poppleton scrolled up from the bottom of the screen:

> NATE: DO NOT RETURN. NOT SAFE. THERE WAS A LEAK. PLAN HAS BEGUN. MUST COMPLETE MISSION. DON'T TRUST—

The message ended abruptly, as if Poppleton hadn't had a chance to type the last word.

I could barely speak as I read the message to Lucy. "It's from Poppleton. He says not to return. There was a leak, and the Syndicate plan has started. He's telling us to complete the mission."

Lucy slumped to the ground as I read her the message. She looked just as stunned as I felt.

If the plan was already in motion, we both knew it meant that the Institute itself—our fellow agents, the computer system, even Red Station—already may have been under the control of the Syndicate.

Knowing this, and knowing that it had happened because of a traitor in our midst, sent a sick feeling coursing through my entire body. My mind raced to put together an explanation, but I could not. *Clearly, someone had told the enemy agents where we would meet Professor Wilson. But who? Who would do something like that to the Institute? Who would put all those agents at risk? And, for that matter, why?*

All I knew at that point was that the only hope The Institute had, the only hope our country had, of avoiding a future controlled by the bad guys lay with Lucy and me.

We had to complete our mission. And we had to do it alone, without the help of the Institute. As I looked at Lucy through the greenish tint of my spy specs I could see she had arrived at the same conclusion.

"What does he say about the mission?" Lucy asked. "Does he tell us how to finish? I thought the mission was to get information from Professor Wilson, and we haven't even done that yet."

"He doesn't say," I said. "He just says 'don't trust' but then it ends."

"It ends?"

"Yeah, like he was going to type someone's name but didn't have time," I said.

"Oh!" Lucy sat bolt upright. "He knows who the traitor is! That must be it!"

"Yeah." I nodded as I slumped to the ground next to her. That had to be it. "But that doesn't do us any good, does it? I wish he had told us the name, or at least how to proceed."

"Well, that would have been nice," Lucy said. "But I guess we'll need to figure out what's next."

We sat in silence for several more minutes.

The anticipation we felt earlier this morning was gone, melted away by the events of the past hour. All that was left was the cold realization that being an agent was deadly serious.

In the hushed silence of the old tunnel, sitting on a cloud of cobwebs and with a sick feeling in my stomach, I began a mental scoreboard: Syndicate 1, Nate and Lucy 0.

7. THE TRAITOR

We had to act. It was one of the first things they taught us at the Institute. When you encountered a setback, you had to act and act quickly. It never helped to wallow in self-pity, second-guessing, or wishful thinking. To be successful, an agent had to persevere, rise to the occasion, show grit.

At least, that was what they taught us.

But it was easier to say than to do.

Sitting there on the cold, dirt floor of the old tunnel, the last thing I felt like doing was showing grit. I felt more like giving up. Knowing that the Syndicate had convinced one of our fellow agents to betray us, and that we couldn't count on The Institute to protect us, left me feeling hollow, alone, and hopeless.

Then there was the cold.

They didn't teach us about the cold in the old tunnels, not in Underground History class or in any other class. But it was definitely cold.

It made sense if you thought about it. The builders back then had very little to work with. Plus, the city itself was still under construction when they dug some of these old tunnels.

Modern builders were able to tap into existing buildings. That was why the new tunnels weren't as cold:

many of them were connected to heating systems from the buildings above.

As Lucy and I sat shivering, with our teeth chattering and our fingers becoming numb, I reminded myself to bring this up with my Underground History teacher.

Lucy was the first to break the silence. "We need to complete the mission."

I knew she was right. As much as I felt like giving up, I knew that we needed to keep going. The fate of the Institute and of our families depended upon it. I couldn't let them down. It was time for me to show some grit.

I nodded as we stood and brushed the cobwebs from our clothing. "I wish Poppleton had told us how. I was hoping we could figure it out back at The Institute."

Lucy smiled and nodded. "Maybe we go back and try to find Professor Wilson?"

I was about to reply when I heard the footsteps.

They weren't the cautious footsteps of agents being careful. These footsteps were loud, making a repeated *clomp clomp* sound that echoed throughout the length of the tunnel. They were coming from the direction of the Red Line.

And they were getting closer.

A situation like this didn't require much conversation. Even though we were close to the Institute, we couldn't be sure who was coming our way. Whoever it was, they probably weren't on our side.

"Quick, this way," I said to Lucy as I motioned deeper into the tunnel, back the way we had come.

We began with a quick and quiet walk, trying to make progress without making any noise. I wondered if Lucy's heart was pounding as fast as mine. If it was, she didn't show it. She looked determined.

It soon became obvious that a quick walk wouldn't do the job. The footsteps were getting closer, maybe 20 yards behind us, just around a slight bend in the tunnel.

If the people attached to those feet got any closer, they would be able to see us. Assuming, that is, they had some sort of night vision technology like we did. And at the speed they were running, I assumed that they did.

Lucy must've been thinking the same thing because, before I could say anything, she slapped me in the chest and broke into a run. Apparently a chest slap was some sort of universal code for "let's run."

So we ran, following the twists and turns in the tunnel, waving our hands in front of us to clear any cobwebs that remained. It must have been quite a sight. Two kids, running in the dark with strange-looking glasses on their faces, waving their arms in the air in front of them.

It was the sort of thing that might have ended up on YouTube if someone with a camera had been in that tunnel. I pictured my friends, gathered around a cell phone, giggling while the video played. But there were no cameras, and Lucy and I certainly didn't think it was funny. For us, it was deadly serious.

It took us only minutes to retrace our steps back to the spot where we had entered the tunnel. We stopped for a moment, listening as the footsteps got closer. Running had given us a few extra seconds, but we didn't have time to open the hatch and get through without being discovered.

And, in any case, we had no way of knowing that the other side of the hatch offered a chance of escape. It was just as likely that Agent Blue was roaming the subway tunnel on the other side waiting for us.

The only option was to continue deeper into the tunnel.

Within a few steps, it became clear that travel would be slow. The tunnel in this direction was narrower and was littered with piles of dirt and debris, like a narrow obstacle course that wound through a fog of cobwebs. We had to slow to a walk, carefully picking our way through the piles of dirt while swatting at the cobwebs.

I was leading the way, waving my arms in front of me as I kept my focus on the ground to avoid tripping over a pile of debris. I had settled into something of a routine. It involved looking down, waving twice, and looking up again. I had followed that routine for a dozen steps until, as I was looking down at the ground, my second wave hit something solid.

I stopped in my tracks as Lucy bumped into me from behind. We had run into a dead end and were surrounded by walls on three sides. And the footsteps behind us were getting closer.

I looked around in a panic. I could see the walls on three sides and the tunnel stretching out behind us. The floor beneath us was hidden beneath a fog of cobwebs.

That was when it hit me: the cobwebs weren't an obstacle, they were an opportunity.

"Quick, down on the ground and then roll against the wall," I whispered as I motioned Lucy down with one hand.

It worked just as I had expected. As Lucy dropped to the ground and rolled to the edge of the tunnel, she disappeared beneath a fog of cobwebs. Even when I looked straight at her, knowing she was there, I couldn't see her.

"What am I doing down here?" Lucy whispered from beneath the screen of cobwebs.

"You're hiding," I said as I dropped to the ground and rolled next to her, pinning her against the wall.

Within seconds, the footsteps were next to me.

There were three sets of feet moving past my head one loud footstep at a time. I braced myself for what would come next, knowing that it would be only seconds before they encountered the end of the tunnel.

We heard the loud smack of flesh against dirt before we heard the voice.

"Ouch," said the voice in a frustrated tone. I was stunned when I heard it. It was a familiar voice, a voice I had heard many times at the Institute, a voice I had heard most recently less than an hour before.

It was Lenny.

At first, the sound of a familiar voice, even a voice I didn't much trust, was reassuring. It was a natural response, I suppose. At that point, pretty much any contact with the Institute or with other agents would have comforted me.

When I thought about it for a second, though, the feeling of comfort turned to a sense of danger. After all,

I hadn't had much time to think about who might have betrayed us, but I realized in a flash that Lenny was one of the prime candidates. I knew that I couldn't stand up and greet him. Even though he was a fellow agent, I couldn't trust him. He might be the double agent.

It took only seconds for me to realize that I was right to be suspicious.

The three people were standing only a few feet from us. I could have reached out and touched their legs as they stood together in that narrow tunnel.

"I don't see any place here where they might have escaped," Lenny said as his feet turned a slow circle. "They must've gone back through the hatch. They won't get far. Ivan is over there with his Syndicate team. They'll stop them."

"Okay," said a voice belonging to one of the other sets of legs. "Let's get back then. We need to prepare. Should be only a few hours now."

Everything was becoming clear. Lenny was the double agent. He was the one who had betrayed us, and now he was helping the Syndicate with their plan.

The very thought of it sent electric chills up and down my spine. To think that one of our own, an agent of the Institute, was giving information to our enemies would have been unthinkable just an hour ago. But now it seemed very real, and the thought of it left me both angry and scared.

An overwhelming sense of rage spread throughout my body as I resisted the urge to jump to my feet. I was not a violent person, but at that moment I felt capable of violence. I imagined how it would feel to punch

Lenny in the face, to see him stagger back in pain, to watch blood dripping from his nose. At that moment, it was what I wanted to do more than anything.

But I knew better. I knew that, even though he had betrayed us, Lenny was insignificant. Even if I attacked him and left him deep in the bitter cold of the old tunnel, the Syndicate's plan would continue. Harming Lenny might make me feel better, but it wouldn't help the mission. All it would do at that point was place us and the mission at risk.

I stayed motionless and silent, trying to keep my teeth from chattering and restraining my deepest impulses to pounce. Soon, the footsteps of the three enemy agents faded into the distance, leaving Lucy and I behind in the cold silence of the tunnel, both of us still stunned by the fact that we had been betrayed by a fellow agent.

We were both silent for a full minute. There was nothing to say, really. We knew where we stood: the Institute would soon be under attack if it wasn't already. We couldn't rely on Poppleton or any of our fellow agents for help. One of the mission leaders was a traitor and was working with the Syndicate. In short, we were in a tough spot. But as frustrating as it all was, sitting around and talking about it wasn't going to help anything. We needed to act.

It was time to complete the mission.

"I guess we need to look at that piece of paper that Professor Wilson gave me," I said wearily. If we couldn't find a clue there, then things were truly hopeless. After all, making contact with Professor Wilson was the entire reason for our mission in the first place.

"Yeah, that sounds right," Lucy replied as she sat up and wiped the cobwebs from her hair. "He sure was right about that Ivan guy. Maybe he left us some other kind of message, too."

I dug his business card from my pocket. If he had given it to me, it must have been some sort of clue. Not enough to stop the takeover, perhaps, but at least *something* to give us direction. That was all we needed at that point. Just some direction. Any direction, really.

The front of the card was simple and didn't contain an address or phone number:

PROFESSOR BILL WILSON
DEPARTMENT OF COMPUTER SCIENCE

It was odd, really. I had never seen a business card without contact information on it. What was the point of that?

Lucy was looking over my shoulder. "Turn it over," she said. "There must be something on the other side."

And sure enough, on the other side of the card was a series of garbled letters:

EXLOGLQJ DW ORFDWLRQ ILIWHHQ
HLJKWB VHYHQ, URRP WZHOYH RQH
IRXU SRLQW ILYH

It was a secret message of some sort. We stared at it for a full minute. Secret messages like this required a key. That was the way secret messages worked. They were converted from the original text to encoded text using some underlying system or key. Only those who knew the key could convert them back and unlock the meaning of the secret message.

Usually an agent knew in advance what the key would be. Without knowing what key Professor Wilson intended us to use, we could have spent years trying to figure out the meaning of the message. Surely he would have known that.

So why hadn't he told me the key?

Then I realized that perhaps he *had* told us the key.

He knew from the start that we were being watched. He probably suspected that someone was eavesdropping. He would have considered all those things when trying to communicate with us and probably disguised the message so that only we would be able to figure it out.

"We need a key, but I can't figure out if he gave us one," I said to Lucy.

"Yeah, he was chattering on about science projects and then, oh!" She grabbed my arm. "That's it! Remember what he said about the picture?"

I thought for a moment before it came to me. "Yes, he said to pair the picture up with the card or something like that. I thought it sounded funny when he said it. Do you have the picture?"

Lucy was already scrolling through the menus on her cell phone. She held the screen so we both could see. It was an unremarkable photo. I had to look at it twice before I noticed anything unusual.

"Look at his right arm," I said to Lucy as she narrowed the focus to show his right arm hanging in front of his right pocket. "He is signaling the key to us right there."

She nodded as she saw the same thing I did. Professor Wilson, his right arm hanging casually by his side, was holding out three fingers on his right hand. It couldn't have been an accident.

"Three fingers," Lucy said. "That has to be just a Caesar shift."

"Of course," I said. "A Caesar shift."

I felt silly for not recognizing it immediately. A Caesar shift was about the simplest system of encryption we had learned. It was a substitution cipher that involved replacing each letter in the original message with a letter that was before it or after it in the alphabet by a certain number of places. So, for example, if the key was right 1 letter, then A would be converted to B in the enciphered message, and B to C, and so on.

In this case, Professor Wilson must have intended to communicate that the key to deciphering the message was to convert it back from a right 3 substitution pattern.

"Okay, so an A in the original message converts to what?" I asked Lucy, knowing the answer but keeping it to myself to double check. This was the way we were trained: partners figured it out independently. Then they checked their work by comparing results.

"D," Lucy said. "And B would convert to what?"

"E."

"Okay, so let's work through this. That first letter, E, would convert back to what?"

"B," I said. "And the X would convert to what?"

"U."

We continued like this for a few minutes, going back and forth over each letter until finally we had deciphered the secret message:

BUILDING AT LOCATION FIFTEEN
EIGHTY SEVEN, ROOM TWELVE ONE
FOUR POINT FIVE

Lucy began entering the location in her TL. Before long she squeezed her face in frustration.

"It won't recognize that room number," she said. "I'm just going to enter 1214. He must have made a mistake with the .5. I have never seen an address or room number with a .5 before."

"And you'd better look for a route that stays away from the zip line tunnels." I was trying hard to hide the worry in my voice but not doing a very good job. "They might be watching those."

I needn't have said anything. Lucy was a step ahead of me.

"Okay, it isn't all that far. It looks like there is an access point for another one of the old tunnels right here." Lucy pointed toward one of the piles of dirt. "Maybe an hour without the zip lines. That's assuming none of these old tunnels have collapsed."

"And that we don't end up buried in cobwebs," I said, thinking I could lighten the mood. But neither of us felt like chuckling.

As we dug through the pile of dirt to reach the access point on the other side, our situation slowly sunk in. The Institute, our fellow agents, and even our families were in danger. Their safety rested on Lucy and me completing our mission.

And we could trust no one.

It wasn't a great feeling.

We stood and took one last, longing look toward the intersection of the old tunnel and the Red Line. Hours ago it was the way to safety. But now, we both knew without having to say it, there was no safety. Not there or anywhere. Not unless we completed our mission.

So we tightened the straps on our mission packs and walked into the cold, cobwebby darkness on the other side of the access point.

8. THE SURPRISE

It took us more than an hour to arrive at the building. Travel was slow in the old tunnels. They were narrow, with odd curves and occasional debris piles. Every so often our route was blocked by a collapsed tunnel or, in one case, a sagging sewer line that we had to crawl under.

The trip was only half the battle. We knew that the difficult and dangerous part would be making our way from the lowest basement of the building to our destination, room 1214, without being discovered

"I think this is it," Lucy said as she crouched in front of the open end of a pipe about as big around as a car tire. "This will drop us under the elevator shaft."

I hesitated for a moment. For one thing, I wasn't a fan of crawling through pipes. For another thing, I didn't think that actually *trying* to get into an elevator shaft seemed like a great idea. It seemed more like the kind of thing an evil villain would do to a hero in a movie.

But I knew that this was the only way we could achieve our mission. So, I took off my mission pack, slid it into the pipe in front of me, and began crawling, alligator-style, through the pipe until I emerged on the other side, covered in dust and cobwebs.

"Okay," Lucy said as she emerged behind me. "There should be ductwork over here that leads straight up to floor 12. It's steep, but we can crawl it."

"Oh terrific, more crawling," I said with a grin.

Lucy wasn't in a laughing mood. She gasped as she pointed to the far wall. "Uh-oh. That looks like a problem."

I saw what she meant right away. The duct was there all right, and it would have been a great plan except for one thing: welded to the opening of the duct, as if to prevent a prisoner from escaping, was a steel grate. We would never get through that.

"Great," I said, looking around for other openings. "Now what?"

Lucy sat down, stunned. "I don't know. Somehow we have to get 12 floors up there."

My gaze followed the wall up until it faded into the darkness. The elevator shaft was so tall even my spy specs weren't powerful enough to make the top visible. But I saw as much as I needed to.

"Look," I said as I pointed to the wall. "There is a vent on every floor, right next to the elevator doors. I bet we can get in that way."

It looked difficult. The wall was completely vertical, with no ladder or grips of any sort. We would have to use our suction handles for climbing.

Problem was, I left one of my suction handles on top of a subway car. It was probably still there, traveling through the subway tunnels at high speed, invisible to all the passengers inside, but a small reminder of how close Lucy and I had already come to a fatal end.

Suction handles were designed to work in pairs. You held onto one while releasing the other and moving it further up the wall. With only one handle, there was nothing to hold on to while moving the handle up the wall. We didn't call that climbing. We called it hanging. Or worse, falling.

Lucky for us, though, Lucy still had both of her suction handles, making three between both of us. We could make it work. Of course, we didn't have much choice.

With our mission packs on our backs, we started the slow process of climbing. We had trained for this. Every agent had. Lucy started by placing a suction handle on the wall as high as she could reach. Using the remaining two handles, I climbed to a position just above where she was hanging, making sure she could reach the lower of my two handles. Then I hung from the top handle while she used the two bottom handles to climb to a position above me.

It was slow at first, but soon we developed a rhythm and made steady progress up the wall. Lucy counted as we passed each floor until, after no time at all, we reached the twelfth floor.

We hung from the suction cups in front of the vent. When I looked through it, I could see room 1214 directly across the deserted hallway.

I nodded at Lucy and examined the vent cover. It was attached with simple tension pins. A bit of pressure or a hard knock from a hand or fist and it would pop out, leaving a small space for us to crawl through.

My body surged with adrenaline as I released my grip on one of the suction handles and prepared to pound my palm against the vent cover. It had been a long day, with a lot of frustration, and the thought of finally succeeding at something was exhilarating. I tensed my body and swung my hand against the vent cover, watching as it clattered to the hallway on the other side.

It took only a few seconds for us to crawl through, replace the vent cover, and walk across the hall to room 1214.

Once we arrived in the room, we were immediately disappointed. It was an empty supply closet.

I had expected some obvious clue, something that would give us direction. But there was nothing even remotely clue-like in that room. It was just an ordinary supply closet.

I began to doubt our plan. Surely Professor Wilson wouldn't have directed us to an empty supply closet, not if he truly wanted to help us.

Thinking we must have missed something in the code, I reached into my pocket to look at his business card again. I checked the code a second time. Then a third time. Just to be sure, I checked it a fourth time. Every time I came out with the same number: 1214.5. It hadn't changed.

Baffled, I walked up and down the hallway with Lucy.

There was a room 1214.

There was a room 1215.

But there was no door between them. And when I stood directly in between them and stared at the wall, I saw nothing.

Nothing, that is, except a fire extinguisher box with the words "break glass in case of emergency" stenciled across the front. It was located on the wall directly between room 1214 and 1215. In fact, if there had been a room 1214.5, the doorway would have been right where that fire extinguisher was.

Now, in a normal situation I would have paused to let my brain work. Usually, if I gave my brain enough time, it could make sense of almost anything. In this particular situation, there were a lot of things my brain might have accomplished if I had given it a chance.

It might have realized that we had been sent to a room number that didn't exist for a good reason.

It might have realized the significance of the fire extinguisher box labeled "break glass in case of emergency."

It might have realized that it had been missing something all along.

But this wasn't a normal situation, and just one glance over my shoulder was enough to tell me that I didn't have time to pause and give my brain time to realize any of those things. Sorry about that, brain.

At that moment, my attention was focused on the numbers above the elevator. Like almost every elevator I had ever seen, this one had a display above it showing what floor the elevator was on. What caught my attention at that moment was that the number was changing from a 6 to a 7.

Someone was in the elevator and was coming this way.

I froze in place. We couldn't afford to be discovered. If there were agents of the Syndicate on that elevator, we would be in grave danger. And even if it were someone like a security guard, a custodian, or even an office worker, our mission would be in jeopardy. After all, any responsible adult who discovered two kids wandering the hallways of an office building would probably start asking questions. They might even call building security or even the police. We didn't have time to deal with that.

The elevator was now at floor 9.

"Quick, we need to go." I looked around the hallway but saw no place to hide. We had only seconds before the elevator doors opened and, possibly, revealed our presence to enemy agents.

Lucy was already a step ahead of me. She was on the ground in front of the vent cover, prying it off with both hands.

The elevator was now at floor 10.

In one motion, Lucy grabbed a suction handle from her pack and dropped feet first into the open vent. Within seconds she was dangling from the suction handle just beneath the opening.

The elevator was now at floor 11.

I rushed to get my suction handle out of my pack, but I was in such a hurry that I forgot to unzip the pack far enough. As I tried to pull the handle out it got stuck, half in and half out, wedged so tightly in the zippered opening that I could no longer budge it, or open the zipper any further.

It wasn't the first time this sort of thing had happened to me.

It happened once at lunch when I tried to pull a bag of chips out of my lunchbox too fast.

It happened once before soccer practice when I tried to pull my zippered sweatshirt over my head without unzipping it far enough. I ended up practicing with a sweatshirt stuck around my head.

It happened once before the district track meet, when I tried to pull my sweats off over my left shoe without unzipping the opening far enough. I ran that race with one leg stuck in sweatpants. It didn't go well.

In those cases, the consequences were pretty minor. Getting locked out of a bag of chips, playing soccer with a sweatshirt for a hat, and hobbling around the track with sweatpants dangling from one ankle were funny and frustrating but not all that serious, really.

This situation was serious. Deadly serious.

The elevator was now at floor 12.

And it was stopping.

"Nate, hurry," Lucy said as she held her suction handle with both hands.

I barely had time to throw my pack over my back before the elevator doors opened. With the vent cover in my left hand, I slid feet first into the opening, holding on to Lucy's handle with one hand while I pulled the vent cover over the opening with the other.

From my position, I couldn't see into the hallway. All Lucy and I could do was keep listening as footsteps emerged from the elevator and walked to the area of the hallway where we had been only seconds before. I couldn't tell if they were the footsteps of enemy agents or simple office workers walking back to their office.

Until, that is, one of them spoke.

"Room 1214 is what they were searching for." It was Lenny. "Must not be here yet. Probably still wandering around underground. Or maybe they gave up, and now they're hiding."

I felt the anger return. But this time, instead of feeling like I wanted to confront him, I felt like I wanted to complete the mission. That was what would feel good.

My grip on the handle was beginning to loosen as a tired ache spread through my forearm. After the adventure on the subway car and the climb up the elevator shaft, my arms and the rest of my body were tired. We trained for missions like this, sure. But we didn't train for *this* much hanging from suction handles. We weren't monkeys, after all.

"I wouldn't dismiss them." I knew the gravelly voice without even looking. Agent Blue. Just a few minutes on the subway with the guy were enough for me to remember his voice forever. "You were pretty sure you had them cornered in the tunnels, too, if I remember correctly, right?"

It was a perfect comeback, putting Lenny in his place without even a hint of emotion. I had to keep myself from laughing out loud. Even though I couldn't see him, I imagined Lenny's face slowly turning pink as he blushed in embarrassment.

"I wonder why they were coming here, though," continued Agent Blue. "Doesn't seem to be much in the way of clues."

I couldn't really say I was shocked by any of it. Hearing Agent Blue didn't shock me. Hearing Lenny there with him, and knowing that Lenny had betrayed us, didn't shock me. Even the fact that they had known where to find us didn't shock me (although, if I had taken the time to think about it, perhaps it should have).

What shocked me was the voice I heard next.

"Well, if they were coming here it must have been for a good reason. Those kids are sharp."

Goosebumps formed on my arms and legs before the last word escaped from her lips. My stomach sank, and I could feel Lucy let out a long but quiet gasp. This was a voice we both knew very well. It was the voice of some-one we trusted in a way that we never trusted Lenny. It was the voice belonging to someone who was just the kind of agent each of us aspired to be.

It was Isabel.

And hearing her voice made me want to cry.

No longer able to resist looking, I slowly raised my head to peer through the vent, hoping that no one was looking in my direction. It was a risk, but I needn't have worried. The three of them stood directly between room 2014 and room 2015.

As I stared at the three enemy agents standing in front of the fire extinguisher box labeled "break glass in case of emergency," a realization hit me like a bolt of lightning. We weren't sent there to find a room at all. We were sent there to find something that was *not* a room. Something that was placed *between* two rooms. Some-thing exactly like a fire extinguisher box, conveniently labeled "break glass in case of emergency."

They were the same words Poppleton had described in our conversation. I suddenly was sure that whatever Professor Wilson had sent us to find, whatever was required to stop the Syndicate's evil plan, was inside that box.

Unfortunately, there were enemy agents standing right next to the box. And if any one of them discovered what was inside, our mission would be over.

"We need to get you out of here before anyone sees you," Agent Blue said to Isabel. "Lenny's cover is blown, but you—you can still pass for a loyal agent of the Institute, right?"

Lenny was casually running his hand along the edge of the box, as if any second he might decide to rip the box from the wall, discover the clue, and destroy any hope we might have of defeating the Syndicate.

Isabel removed the danger by ushering Lenny and Agent Blue toward the elevator. "Yeah, that's right. Let's get out of here. You should put agents at every entry point down below. That way if they are trying to get in, you can capture them."

"And what if they're hiding?" asked Lenny.

"It won't matter. The lights go out at 6, and the attack starts at 7. If they haven't completed their mission by then, it will be too late. By that time, the Institute will be defenseless. That's when we start going after the other agents."

"And their families?" asked Lenny.

Isabel hesitated. "Yes. Yes, and their families," she said in a hushed tone, as if she regretted that she had to say it.

Then they stepped into the elevator, and they were gone.

As the elevator doors closed behind them I felt both relief and a deep, gut-wrenching fear. Relief that the Institute hadn't yet been attacked. Fear that the Institute, all my fellow agents, and even my own family were in grave danger.

Isabel's words echoed in my mind. *The lights go out at 6, and the attack starts at 7.* I glanced at my watch. It was 4 PM.

We had only three hours to stop them.

9. THE CHIP

The early-evening light filtered through the window shades on the twelfth floor as my mind drifted to thoughts of basketball practice. It wasn't unusual for my mind to wander, but in this case I was thinking of basketball practice for a very specific reason: it was our cover story.

You see, basketball practice at the Institute wasn't real. It was phony. Fake. Fictional. We didn't schedule basketball practices in order to actually, you know, practice basketball. We did it to provide a cover story to our parents when we needed extra time to complete missions. It was no different from band practice, math club, or the occasional field trip.

It was all part of keeping The Secret. Some missions took all day, and our parents wouldn't have approved of a school day that lasted until 8 PM. That was too much school for anyone. Our parents weren't crazy, after all. So we needed to create reasons for staying at school so late.

Of course, if there wasn't a mission to complete, we simply did our homework or got some exercise. We never wasted time, and we never did anything our parents wouldn't have approved of. Assuming that our parents would have approved of us being spies.

Anyway, that was what I was thinking as Lucy and I hung in the elevator shaft: thank goodness I had basketball practice scheduled so that my parents wouldn't show up at the Institute and find out I was gone.

"Nate, I can't hold on for much longer," said Lucy as she struggled to maintain her grip on the handle. I could tell her arms were as tired as mine.

"I know. We need to get back in the hallway." I pounded against the back of the vent cover until it clattered to the ground. With my hands grasping the edges of the opening, I climbed into the hallway, and then reached behind me to help Lucy. "Here, you can grab my hand."

"I guess I need to train more or something," Lucy said as she pulled herself through the opening. "All that hanging makes my arms feel like gummi worms."

"Yeah, I hear you," I said as I strode toward the fire extinguisher box. I knew exactly what I needed to do. Without saying anything to Lucy, I slowly and carefully worked my zip handle free of my mission pack and swung it at the glass cover of the fire extinguisher.

Lucy let out a slight shriek as the glass shattered and particles scattered everywhere.

"Nate, what are you doing?"

"It's this box," I said. "This box is room 1214.5."

I wasn't sure what I was looking for, but I knew it was in that box. Being careful of the broken glass, I reached inside and pulled out the fire extinguisher. There were no unusual marks on the sides of it. And, with the fire extinguisher removed, the box was completely empty.

Puzzled, I ran my hand along the back of the box. There weren't any secret compartments that I could tell, and there certainly weren't any messages. I was about to put the fire extinguisher back in the box when I noticed something taped to the bottom that made my heart race.

It was an envelope.

I carefully removed it, put the fire extinguisher back in the box, and walked over to sit in one of the lobby chairs.

It felt good to sit down. The chase on the subway train, trouncing through the old tunnel, climbing the elevator shaft, and hanging from the suction handles had taken their toll. I was exhausted.

But this was no time to rest. Just the opposite. This was a time to hurry.

I examined the envelope, turning it over in my hand to look at all sides of it. I resisted the impulse to tear it open. They taught us at the Institute to examine first, think second, and act third. Acting first, Poppleton always liked to say, could often lead to regretting second and something even worse third.

It was a small red envelope, the color of the fire extinguisher and the size of a playing card. There was no writing and there were no marks on it, but the contents created a small bulge in the envelope, as if a small Lego piece were hidden inside.

Satisfied that I wouldn't ruin anything by opening it, I slowly tore off one side, tilted the open end toward my palm, and watched as a small object landed in my hand.

It was a small rectangle. Flat and black on one side, it had a set of tiny black wires protruding from the other side. I knew what it was as soon as I saw it.

"It's a microchip," blurted out Lucy, stealing my thunder.

She was right. We studied these in Computer Espionage class. Every computer had one. Even cell phones and televisions had them. Pretty much every electronic device had a microchip of some sort in it. Without microchips, none of those devices would work.

I suddenly realized what Agent Blue had been after on the subway train. When he yelled, "Where's the chip?" he wasn't talking about potato chips. He was talking about a microchip.

"This is the chip," I said. "This is the chip he was talking about."

"What do you mean?" Lucy said.

"On the train. When he kept yelling 'Where's the chip?' he meant a computer chip."

"Ah," Lucy nodded. "I wonder what it does."

"I don't know, but I'm guessing if they're working that hard to get it, they must know. Maybe it's something we can use to stop their plan," I said.

"I hope so," Lucy said. "Man, it sure would've been nice if Professor Wilson had told us what to do with it. Hey, how did you think to break the glass like that, anyway? I don't remember him saying anything about that."

Lucy's question reminded me about the envelope that Poppleton had given me. It was the whole point of his "break the glass" comment. He had said to open it if

99

there was an emergency. Well, if anything qualified as an emergency, I was pretty sure the Institute being under attack did.

I had it out of my pocket in only seconds. "For Nate and Lucy" was written in large block letters on each side of the envelope. The only unusual thing was the spacing. There was extra space inserted between some of the letters, as if Poppleton had been in such a hurry when he wrote it that he hadn't made sure that the letters were evenly spaced.

I didn't think much of it. I was in a hurry to see the message.

Lucy was a different story, though. When I removed the letter and handed her the empty envelope, I could tell she was already trying to decide what shape she wanted to fold with it. Deciding what shape she wanted to make was usually her biggest challenge.

The plain white sheet of paper contained a short, handwritten note:

NATE,

IF YOU ARE READING THIS, THE VIRUS HAS SPREAD. ONLY YOU AND LUCY CAN STOP IT. TELL LUCY TO GET OFF THE FENCE AND FOLD A SWAN. TCTEV IOTCC INOVR XVOLI TOTUI NTLAT IDBUA HOUET MEIEL GMEOS EOATH MECLO WDBHR OEGKI TNRYP REBDR FZSER MCIEP RYLWI ILEUN CHEPH ISCUS NUIOI EIRRP ENCUL WKILS EVSTA T.

BE SAFE, POPPLETON

I looked at the garbled end of the message for a full minute. Obviously it was a secret message, but we had to figure out how to decipher it. The last line that made sense was, "Tell Lucy to get off the fence and fold a swan." It must have been a clue. Poppleton didn't write something like that without a good reason.

"What do you think, should I fold a swan?" Lucy asked. "I kind of wanted to fold this envelope into something, anyway. I wonder how Poppleton knew."

"Go for it," I said. I didn't wonder how Poppleton knew. Anyone who knew even the slightest bit about Lucy would have known that she would want to fold that envelope into a shape. That part was clear. What wasn't clear was why we needed a paper swan.

"Oh, look!" Lucy had already folded the envelope into the shape of a tiny swan and was pointing at it. "Look at the wings. There's a new word!"

Sure enough, after all the different folds had been made, the letters were rearranged and across the top of the swan was a line of four letters making a simple word: "FOUR."

I immediately checked to see if the number four was a simple clue indicating a Caesar shift. I tried deciphering the message using every key connected to the number four I could think of. I tried substituting for each letter the letter that was four letters before it in the alphabet and four letters after. The message was still garbled. I tried substituting four letters before in the alphabet and four letters after, then reading the message backwards. It still didn't make sense. I tried everything I could think of and nothing worked.

"I don't think this is a Caesar shift at all," I said, baffled.

"Yeah, I can't make it work, either," Lucy said, looking over my shoulder. "What's that mean, 'tell Lucy to get off the fence,' anyway?"

I looked at the sentence again:

> TELL LUCY TO GET OFF THE FENCE AND
> FOLD A SWAN.

At first I thought "get off the fence" just meant "make a decision." But Poppleton could have written, "Tell Lucy to fold a swan," and it would have meant the same thing. He included four extra words that weren't really necessary. At least, they weren't necessary unless he was trying to tell us something. Like maybe what kind of code or cipher we were dealing with.

"Fence!" I said as I realized why he had included the four words. "That's the hint about what kind of cipher this is! It's a rail fence cipher!"

"Of course," Lucy said. "Why else would he put that bit in there about me getting off the fence? That must be it."

A wave of relief spread through my body as I began to decipher the message. We learned about rail fence ciphers in Codes class. All of the letters in the original message were just rearranged to form a new message. We called it a transposition cipher.

It usually worked this way: The person converting the original message would decide how many rows to convert it into. Then, the letters from the original message would be placed in order row-by-row; so, the first letter in the first row, the second letter in the second row, and on and on until each row had one letter. Once each row had a letter, the process would continue starting back at the first row. Then the rows would be combined into one long string of text.

The key to deciphering the message was to know how many rows the original message had been placed in, and Poppleton had told us on Lucy's swan: four. That meant that the letters in the original message had been rearranged into four rows of text.

We began deciphering the message using a pencil Lucy pulled from her mission pack.

"Okay, we need to break this into four lines of text," I said. "Should be 34 letters on each line I think."

Lucy scrawled the lines on the side of the origami swan:

TCTEVIOTCCINOVRXVOLITOTUINTLATIDBU
AHOUETMEIELGMEOSEOATHMECLOWDBHROEG
KITNRYPREBDRFZSERMCIEPRYLWIILEUNCH
EPHISCUSNUIOIEIRRPENCULWKILSEVSTAT

"So, first letter of each line makes T-A-K-E," Lucy said.

"And the second letter makes C-H-I-P," I continued.

Before long, we had the entire message converted:

TAKECHIPTOTHEUNIVERSITYCOMPUTERSCIE
NCEBUILDINGROOMFIVEZEROSIXSERVERRO
OMPLACEITINTHECOMPUTERLUCYWILLKNO
WITWILLDISABLETHEVIRUSDONTBECAUGHT

Once we figured out where to put spaces, periods, and even an apostrophe, it ended up like this:

TAKE CHIP TO THE UNIVERSITY.
COMPUTER SCIENCE BUILDING.
ROOM 506.
SERVER ROOM.
PLACE IT IN THE COMPUTER.
LUCY WILL KNOW.
IT WILL DISABLE THE VIRUS.
DON'T BE CAUGHT.

"What does that mean, 'Lucy will know'?" Lucy asked. "I don't feel like I know anything!"

"I don't know. Maybe it will make sense when we get there." I said.

"Well, then," said Lucy. "Let's get this show on the road. I'll tell the TL where we want to go next."

It wasn't so much *what* she said, but *how* she said it: as if she was letting the TL in on a secret that only the two of us knew. She didn't mean anything by it. But it hit me that she was, in fact, sharing a secret. She was telling the TL where we were going next. Only we knew that information, I realized, until she entered it in the TL. Once she entered it, anyone monitoring the TL signals would know also.

That must have been how Agent Blue had tracked us to the subway car, how Lenny and the Syndicate agents had known where to look for us in the tunnel, and how all of them, even Isabel, knew we were headed to room 1214.5 (of course, they thought we were heading to room 1214 because that is what Lucy had searched for). They knew where we were because we had told them where we were. Either they had hacked into the TL system, or Lenny and Isabel found a way to track our TL signals.

"Wait," I said a split second before she had started entering the location. "You can't."

She gave me an irritated look that lasted only a moment before the realization sunk in. Her shoulders slumped. "Oh, man, how could we have been so stupid? Of course. The TL. They're tracking us on the TL. I guess it explains why they are always one step ahead of us. But how are we going to figure out how to get where we need to go?"

"I don't know. We might have to get as close as we can, and then just risk doing a search. All I know right now is that we need to get out of this building."

"No kidding, Einstein," Lucy said with a chuckle. "You have a plan I suppose? It sounds like they're covering all the exits, even the tunnels."

She was right, of course. We couldn't go back the way we had come. It was too dangerous. Agents of the Syndicate would have every tunnel in and out of the basement guarded. If there was a way out, it wasn't through the basement.

We needed to come up with a new plan.

Fortunately, we had covered situations like this in Spy Tactics class. Our teacher, Mrs. Sorkin, was fond of saying, "a battle plan never survives first contact with the enemy." What she meant was that things always changed, even for spies. The key to being a successful spy wasn't to have the best plan, but to respond quickly to any changes that happened. That had been drilled into us from the first day of class. And we were taught tactics to help us respond to situations just like this.

The one that popped into my mind at that moment was what we called, "The Advantage Tactic." It was simple. No matter what the situation, no matter what the location, and no matter who the enemy, it was always possible to identify at least one thing that could be used as an advantage. Sometimes it was intelligence, other times it was speed. I'd even heard stories about agents using hailstorms to their advantage. Any advantage could be used, but the key was being able to recognize it.

At that moment, we obviously didn't have the advantage of using a network of tunnels.

We were outnumbered, so our numbers weren't our advantage.

Knowing Lenny and Isabel, and having seen Agent Blue in action, I doubted that combat skills were our advantage.

No, our advantage was something else; something that was painfully obvious to me after climbing twelve stories up an elevator shaft. Our advantage was that we were up high, and we could go even higher. We were standing in very tall building, a building which stood nestled among even taller buildings, and the enemy agents were all below us.

It was a relief simply to recognize an advantage, to feel like there was hope. I could feel the elation in my voice as I spoke. "We need to get to the roof. Right away."

Lucy nodded. She knew exactly what I was thinking. But the words she uttered as I turned toward the elevator quickly dampened my enthusiasm. "Nate, we can't use the elevator."

She was right. Of course, she was right. Once we stepped on that elevator we would be trapped in a room 6 feet wide by 6 feet long. We would have no control over where it stopped. And, if it stopped on a floor with agents of the Syndicate, we would be finished.

I searched my tired brain for options but could find none. "The roof is like 50 floors above us. We can't climb all that way with the suction cups. Not with my arms feeling the way they do."

"Yeah, no way." Lucy was shaking her head. "But maybe we can use the elevator without actually, you know, using the elevator."

I stared at her blankly, wondering if fatigue or maybe the stress of our situation had made her crazy. Dumbfounded, I repeated the last part of her sentence to make sure I understood what she had said. "Use the elevator without actually using the elevator?"

"Yeah, you know, we can—"

I held up my hand to interrupt her. I felt foolish for not understanding the first time. "Oh, I got it, I got it. Great idea!"

"Okay, so do you want to do the scary part, or do you want me to?" Lucy asked.

"I'll do it. You get attached to the elevator. Here." I worked the zipper loose on my pack, pulled my suction handle free, and handed it to Lucy. "I won't have any need for this."

I tried not to think too much about what we were planning to do. If I thought about it, I would find some excuse not to do it. We couldn't afford that. We had less than two hours to complete our mission. We couldn't afford any hesitation or second thoughts.

Lucy crawled through the vent opening and attached herself to the wall on the side of the elevator shaft. She was in a space just narrow enough to allow her to fit without being crushed by an elevator.

Walking toward the elevator button, I shook my arms to loosen the muscles. It would be the last chance those muscles had to rest for a while.

The number above the elevator on the right-hand side showed the elevator on the first floor. I pushed the elevator button and watched the numbers above the elevator slowly change as the elevator climbed to our floor.

This was the part of the plan that relied on hope. All I could do at that point was hope that when those doors opened, there were no Syndicate agents inside. Because if there were, I had little chance of escape.

The elevator was at floor eight when I realized that we had forgotten something. I pulled the chip from my pocket and raced to the vent opening to hand it to Lucy. "Here, you need to have this in case I get caught."

"Okay, but don't get caught."

I returned to the elevator just as the number changed to 12. It was probably the longest 2 seconds of my life waiting for that door to open. I ran through the possible scenarios in my head. But the one I kept coming back to was this: if there were Syndicate agents in the elevator, I would run down the hallway as fast as I could. That would give Lucy a chance to escape. I owed her that, at least.

When the doors opened, there was nothing there. Just empty space in a dimly lit elevator. I had never been so happy to see empty space. But I didn't have time to celebrate the beauty of unoccupied airspace. I needed to move fast.

With one hand holding the elevator door open, I leaned inside and pressed the highest number I could reach. I didn't even take the time to see what number it was. All I knew was that it was at the top of the panel and would take us as high as that elevator could go.

Before I let the elevator door close, I called out to Lucy. "Are you attached?"

"All set, go for it." Her voice echoed inside the elevator shaft, almost like she was making an announcement at a school assembly.

Still holding the elevator door open, I backed into the hallway, getting myself as close to the vent opening as I possibly could. I needed every advantage I could get.

That was when I noticed it.

In the top left corner of my vision, barely even noticeable from my angle, the number on the second elevator changed to a 12. Silently, sneakily, the second elevator had been climbing while I worked. It was now on the 12th floor, only feet away from me.

And the doors were opening.

I immediately let go of the elevator door and rushed to the vent opening. There was no need to think. If Syndicate agents were on that other elevator, I needed to get away, and get away fast. Otherwise, our mission would be doomed.

I heard them before I saw them. It was Lenny and Agent Blue, and they were carrying on a conversation as the elevator doors opened.

"—won't be able to resist. Maybe Poppleton will hold out for a while, but the rest of them should be easy to capture," Agent Blue said in his gravelly voice.

"What about—" Lenny paused as he saw me in front of the vent opening. "Hey, there he is!"

Despite the danger, I felt confident. I had a head start, after all. All I had to do was slide through the vent opening and our plan would be set in motion.

It was a simple plan, really. While I held the elevator door open so that the elevator would stay on our floor, Lucy had moved her suction handle from the wall of the elevator shaft to the outside of the elevator itself. She was now firmly attached to the elevator. Once I made it through the opening, all I would need to do was grab hold of the same suction handle she was hanging from and hold on as the elevator took off like a rocket ship. Or, at least, like an elevator.

It didn't take long for my confidence to be shaken. As I dove through the opening and reached out for the suction handle, I felt the pocket of my cargo pants catch against the side of the vent opening. That was one thing about cargo pants: they were convenient when you needed extra pockets, but not so great when you were slipping through tight spaces.

So there I was with my upper body inside the elevator shaft, my hand only inches from the suction handle, and my legs hanging out into the hallway.

"Nate, hurry! The elevator's moving!" Lucy shouted. I could see she was right. The suction handle was moving farther away from my outstretched hands. Lucy's eyes widened in fear as first the suction handle, then her shoulders, and finally her outstretched hand moved further away. I had only seconds before she would be completely beyond my reach.

Agent Blue and Lenny were feet away from me as I struggled to free myself. I squirmed and jerked and rolled and kicked. But it was no use. My pocket was firmly stuck.

I had only one option. I reached out and grabbed Lucy's outstretched leg, dug the foot of my free leg into the ground for leverage, and pushed myself through the opening as hard as I could. The tearing of fabric seemed to echo in the hallway as I slid through the opening and into safety. (Or at least the relative safety of hanging from a partner's leg while attached to a rising elevator).

I looked down and saw Lenny's face peering up at me from the opening. But I didn't feel elation. I didn't feel like gloating. I didn't even feel like adding to my mental scoreboard (although, just for the record, if I had it would have read, Syndicate 1, Nate and Lucy 1).

No, I didn't feel any of those things. My attention was drawn to something else, something that on most other days and in most other situations I wouldn't have given a second thought: the second elevator (the one Agent Blue and Lenny had climbed to the twelfth floor, and the one that was probably waiting open for them after I escaped) was making a gentle whirring sound as it began to climb behind us.

10. THE ESCAPE

Our elevator picked up speed as it climbed to the top floor. Lucy clung to its side, and I clung to her leg. My arms were exhausted, and my heart was doing a tap dance inside my chest. If our escape plan didn't work, our mission was doomed and so was the Institute.

Man, talk about pressure.

We knew there was no point in talking as we watched the floors glide by, each one marked by a dimly-illuminated vent cover. Our mission was clear, and so was the danger we faced. It was hard to ignore, really, given that it trailed us in an elevator only five floors below.

I looked up through the dim light of the elevator shaft as we approached the top floor. Against the ceiling, directly above our elevator, was a single door. I knew in an instant that door represented our path to freedom.

There was just one problem: we couldn't reach it.

Lucy hung from the suction handle on the outside of the elevator, too far from the top to climb up. There were no handles or grips on the side of the elevator or on the wall. There was no way she could get in a position to reach that door. Not unless she suddenly turned into a spider.

My position was even worse. I was hanging from Lucy's leg, struggling just to maintain my grip, with my own legs and feet dangling in the empty chasm below the elevator.

More than 50 stories of a narrow, dark, and mostly empty elevator shaft separated us from the cold, hard ground. One mistake and we would be in for a long fall and a very hard landing.

In short, we weren't exactly in the best position to get to the door.

But we didn't have time to complain.

"Climb over me, that's the only way," Lucy said.

She was right. There was no other way. Still, knowing it was the only option didn't make it easy. Climbing over Lucy, holding all of my weight with nothing more to grip than a pair of jeans, a mission pack, and a skinny set of shoulders was easier said than done. But I did it anyway.

From a position atop her shoulders, I reached up and grabbed the top edge of the elevator and hung with both hands, ignoring the arm fatigue and the fear I felt from knowing what was below us.

"Okay, all set," I said. "Better hurry."

My arms trembled as Lucy grabbed my leg and started to climb. By the time she climbed on top of my shoulders I felt like my arms were going to pull out of my shoulder sockets. Seconds later, though, she was on top of the elevator roof and reaching down to help me up.

It was a huge relief to be on top of that elevator, but we had no time to rest. We had to get the door open and reach the roof of the building before Syndicate agents stopped us. Their elevator was only two floors below us. In seconds, it would stop right next to us.

We used all our strength to get the door open only a few feet. It was a struggle. The metal door was heavy, and opening it from below required moving all its weight. I started to realize that opening a door from below wasn't nearly as easy as those characters on *Monsters, Inc.* made it look. At least, not for two agents who had been hanging from an elevator while it climbed more than 50 floors.

While I held the door open about a foot, Lucy climbed through the narrow opening and stood on top of the building's roof. The strain of holding the weight of the door showed in her face. It made sense. After all, she had been holding both my weight and hers as we hung from the elevator. She was probably pretty tired.

"Hurry," she said as she grabbed the door. "I can't hold it for long."

She could have saved her breath. Something else was already making me hurry. The second elevator had stopped and Lenny was crawling out of the small door on its roof. Once he gained his footing, he would be close enough to grab me. And, even once I made it through the doorway, he would be in a perfect position to open the door and follow us.

"Let it close!" I yelled as I scrambled through the doorway and joined Lucy on the roof. "Quick!"

The door slammed shut behind me and Lucy and I were suddenly alone in the quiet, sparkling darkness of the city at night. Light shone from the windows of buildings, from rooftops, and from the street below. It was the sort of scene they made postcards out of.

Of course, we weren't postcard designers. We were spies. And we had more important things to think about.

"Over there." Lucy pointed to a tall, majestic building less than 10 blocks away. I would've recognized it anywhere. It was the Empire State Building, one of the tallest buildings in the city. And it stood before us like an inviting escape route. "The zip line gun. We should be able to make it."

I nodded unconvincingly. The zip line gun was a last resort. It had been in our pack since we started school, but we had never used it. That was because it was only the sort of thing we used in a dire emergency.

It was a pretty simple device. It could shoot a small metal dart, almost like the tip of an arrow that would anchor itself into almost anything. Connected to the dart was an incredibly strong, but also very thin, zip line. When fired at one building, the zip line gun allowed agents to create zip lines that stretched from building to building.

It sounded great in theory, but in practice it was incredibly risky. One slip from the zip handle and an agent could fall to his death.

But we didn't have a choice.

"You get started, I'll stall them," I said as I turned toward the door.

In seconds Lenny and the other agents would try to open that door. If they made it through before Lucy and I escaped on a zip line, we would be finished. I had to buy her enough time to create an escape route for us.

This was just the sort of situation that called for a spy gadget. Maybe something that would have allowed me to weld the door shut, like a small pen with a special laser strong enough to melt metal. Or a wristwatch that shot out superheated flames. At that point, I would have settled for a tube of super-bonding, fast-drying, easy-to-use super glue.

Any of those things would have been great to have at that moment. But I had none of them. All I had was my body, my brain, and a little bit of common sense.

So I used the only substitute I had for a spy gadget: my body weight.

I sat on the door as Agent Blue, Lenny, and their fellow agents pushed on the other side. They struggled to move the door with my weight positioned on top of it. It wasn't that I was all that heavy. I wasn't one of those kids who ate donuts for breakfast and Doritos for lunch. Just the opposite: I was a skinny kid. Still, even a skinny kid sitting on top of a heavy door can be hard to move. Just ask Lenny and Agent Blue.

Lucy made progress in a hurry. She pulled the zip line gun from her mission pack and aimed at the roof of a tall building two blocks away. The gun sparked as the metal dart sailed through the air, pulling the zip line behind it with a whooshing sound. Lucy quickly tied off the other end, and the zip line was ready.

She looked at me expectantly. "Let's go."

"I can't move. They'll break through." I could already feel them making progress as my seat atop the door kept bobbing up and down, first only an inch at a time and then almost a foot at a time. It would be only a few seconds before they held it open far enough for one of them to slip through. I started to wish that I *was* one of those kids who ate donuts for breakfast and Doritos for lunch. "You get to the other side. I'll follow in a second."

I could see from her expression that Lucy wanted to argue, to tell me to stand up and join her. But she knew I was right. So she clipped her handle to the zip line, gave a nod, and disappeared into the darkness.

My zip handle was in my hand when I felt the door rise beneath me. It didn't bob up and down. It just kept rising in one smooth motion, like the agents below had suddenly been joined by a power lifter, or a machine, or even a Wookie. The force of it sent me sprawling and stunned onto the roof of the building as the door clattered all the way open next to me.

I was on my feet in seconds, ready to run to the zip line.

But it was too late. Lenny, Agent Blue, and two agents I had never seen before were already on the roof. One was a man, and one was a woman. Both had short black hair and the man had a stubble of hair on his chin. But more important than their hair color was the fact that both of them looked strong, fit, and deadly serious.

And all of them—Lenny, Agent Blue, and the two dark-haired, strong, fit, and serious agents—were standing between me and the zip line.

My only advantage was that they didn't know about the zip line and, most important of all, they thought Lucy was on the roof with me.

It was time to use The Advantage Tactic.

"Look, we don't want to hurt you," Agent Blue said as he looked around the rooftop, trying to locate Lucy. "We just want the chip, that's all. Then we'll let you go."

It was creepy to hear how easy it was for him to lie. I knew he had no intention of letting us go. That was the last thing he would do. Once he had the chip, both of us would be doomed.

The agents were slowly spreading out, creating a line of agents between me and the zip line. I backed away, toward the edge of the building farthest from the zip line, putting distance between myself and the agents but at the same time getting further and further from my only escape route.

To my left were the outlines of heating ducts, air conditioners, and skylights on the roof of the building. At night they looked like a collection of geometrically-shaped shrubs, like the sort of shrubs that a secret agent might hide in to avoid detection. I knew as soon as I saw them that they were my chance.

"Lucy!" I yelled as I turned and faced the darkened shapes. "They want the chip. Use the zip line. Over the edge!"

Of course, Lucy wasn't hiding among the heating ducts and air conditioners. She wasn't poised to jump over the edge using her zip line. She wasn't even on the roof with me.

But Agent Blue didn't know that. Lenny didn't know that. And the other agents, with their dark hair and fit bodies, certainly didn't know that.

Confused, and certain that they had Lucy cornered, three of them immediately rushed toward the shadows. It was as if I no longer mattered.

It was the perfect deception in every way except one: Agent Blue didn't fall for it. He stood motionless, watching me the way I had seen my cat watching mice. I had fooled the other three, but I hadn't fooled Agent Blue.

"Where is she?" Agent Blue began walking toward me, looking behind me as if he would see a zip line attached there. "She zipped away, right? Where is the line?"

I had one more chance. The three other agents would soon realize that they had been fooled. When they did, my opportunity to escape would be gone. I had to get away while it was just me and Agent Blue, one-on-one, agent against agent.

And I could tell from his voice that I had an opening to trick him. All I needed was a few seconds, one distraction, just a bit of misdirection, and I would be free to join Lucy and zip away into the darkness.

"Over here," I mumbled nervously as I pointed to the right side of the building. "It's over here."

Now, one thing I learned at the Institute was that I was no good at acting. Anyone who asked me to play a part in the school play, or to pretend to be someone I wasn't, was setting me up to fail. Everyone knew it. They didn't call me "No Drama" Nate because I was calm. They called me that because I was no good at Drama class.

But, of course, Agent Blue didn't know that I was no good at acting. Or, I should say, he didn't know that *I knew* that I was no good at acting. As far as Agent Blue knew, I thought I was the best actor in the world.

That was what made my trick effective. I doubted that my acting would fool Agent Blue. My lame attempt to trick him into thinking Lucy was on the right side of the building would only make him think that she wasn't there. He would probably assume that where I really wanted to flee was toward the other side of the building. That was what I was counting on. It was what made my next move that much more effective.

Having set Agent Blue up to expect me to flee to the left side of the building that was exactly what I pretended to do. I did a very lame head fake to the right and took two running steps toward the left side of the building.

I could see immediately that my plan had worked. Agent Blue lunged to intercept me, taking a good three strides before my second stride had landed. If I had really wanted to get to that side of the building I would have failed.

But that wasn't what I wanted. No, what I wanted was exactly what I got: Agent Blue moving at full speed toward the left side of the building, leaving the entire right side of the building open.

It was like watching the clouds part on a sunny day.

Still staring to my left (where the eyes looked was the key to any good deception), I planted hard with my left foot and made a hard cut to my right.

Agent Blue tried to stop, but he was moving so fast that he lost his footing and ended up sliding to the ground. That gave me an opening to run directly between him and the right side of the building. I was maybe 20 steps away from the zip line. All I had to do was get there first, attach my handle to the zip line, and whoosh away into the darkness.

It would have been easier if Agent Blue had stayed on the ground, but he didn't. He was up immediately, running behind me in pursuit.

I gripped the zip handle hard in my right hand as I ran, knowing that it was my only chance at escape. As I came closer to the zip line I could see that I wouldn't have the chance to attach the handle in the slow, deliberate way that I wanted. There would be no time to stop and stand there, making sure everything was secure.

Agent Blue was too close to me, and he was closing fast.

My only advantage at that point, really, was that I knew exactly where the zip line was. I could see where Lucy had tied it to the building and, even though it was pretty much invisible in the darkness, I imagined that I could see its narrow outline against the twinkling lights of the city at night.

At that point there was only one option. I approached the edge of the building at full speed, took one look over my shoulder at Agent Blue as he slowed to avoid toppling over the edge, and I jumped.

It wasn't the helpless jump of an agent giving up.

It wasn't the nervous jump of someone expecting to hit the ground.

It wasn't an aimless jump without any purpose.

No, this was a very deliberate jump. It was a jump made with a plan. And I desperately needed for the plan to succeed.

I sailed into the nighttime darkness, and for a moment, for just a brief moment, time seemed to slow down. The air beneath my feet was filled with the lights and sounds of city traffic. Around me was a sea of buildings and lights amid the still night air. And inside my chest it felt like the tap dance my heart had been performing all night had suddenly stopped.

They taught us at the Institute that every so often an agent encountered a defining moment, a moment when the mission and even the lives of agents hung in the balance, and either success or failure could triumph.

I had no doubt that this was one of those moments. If my plan didn't work, I would fall helplessly to the hard asphalt hundreds of feet below. It would be a long fall but a very short, and very painful, landing. It was, quite literally, a life or death situation.

Normally, this kind of situation would have frightened me. In fact, that very morning I probably wouldn't have thought of a plan like this, let alone actually gone through with it. I probably would have stayed on the roof, cowering in fear, as Agent Blue captured me. But as I sailed through the air I felt my body surge with a kind of confidence I had never felt before.

I knew my plan would work. It had to.

My eyes focused on the narrow zip line. It was almost impossible to see, but I could just barely make it out against the background of window lights. With one motion, I gripped the zip handle with my right hand and reached out to attach it to the zip line. There was a loud click followed by the gentle whirring of the zip handle as I sailed into the darkness toward Lucy and safety, leaving Agent Blue and the other Syndicate agents stranded on the roof behind me.

At least, that was what I thought as I zipped comfortably through the galaxy of office lights in the night sky like the *Millennium Falcon* entering hyperspace. Escaping from Agent Blue made me relaxed and elated at the same time, and I was sure that my escape had guaranteed the success of our mission. I was so sure of it that I updated my mental scoreboard. Syndicate 1, Nate and Lucy 2.

I was wrong.

Only seconds after I had zipped away from the building, there was a sharp jerk on the zip line. It was so strong and unexpected that I nearly lost my grip. When I recovered and looked over my shoulder, I saw shapes outlined against the background of city lights and heard the gentle hum of zip handles behind me. My heart felt like it skipped a beat as I realized what had happened.

The enemy agents had found the zip line, and they were following me.

11. THE CHASE

One thing they taught us at the Institute was to stay calm. No matter how dangerous, hopeless, or stressful things seemed, we were never supposed to get too excited or too worried. They showed us all sorts of techniques that were supposed to make it easy.

There was "meditation for spies." That was a tricky one. Trying to focus on nothing except breathing while being an actual, you know, *spy* wasn't so easy.

There was "distraction by subtraction." We started with a number and subtracted our age over and over again. It was supposed to distract us from our worries, but it usually left me wishing I had a calculator.

There was "imagining a calm place." All it took was thinking of a place that made us feel relaxed, happy, and calm. For some agents that was the ocean, but for me it was my reading tent. Usually, if I thought about my reading tent, calm washed over me like a light fall drizzle.

I tried all the techniques, but none of them worked.

The thing that made me anxious and nervous and angry all at the same time was the fact that I should have seen this coming. I should have known that Agent Blue, Lenny, and the rest of the agents would have zip handles. It made perfect sense. Obviously, Lenny had one. I should have guessed that the others would have them, too.

Our plan had been to get to the top of the Empire State Building without being followed. We thought that once we got there everything would be fine. We would have a vantage point atop the city and could easily zip to any location we wanted, well ahead of the enemy agents who we thought would be chasing us from the street below.

The fact that the enemy agents were following us in the air made things a lot more complicated. They were so close that we wouldn't have time to stop and plan. And, even worse, once we arrived at our destination, they would be close enough to prevent us from completing our mission.

I blamed myself. The fact that I had devised a plan that didn't allow for the possibility that we would be chased in the air was a big mistake. I knew that it would cost me major points during the mission evaluation assembly. I also knew that it was time to adjust the scoreboard. Syndicate 2, Nate and Lucy 2.

The more urgent concern was that they were gaining on us quickly. Every time I looked over my shoulder, they were closer. I hit the turbo setting on my zip handle, but they continued to gain. At the rate they were moving, I knew they would catch me before I arrived at the next building to join Lucy.

I had to do something to slow them. Unfortunately, doing battle while riding on a zip line wasn't something they trained us for at the Institute. They probably assumed there wasn't any need. After all, only agents of the Institute traveled on zip lines, and they would never battle each other. At least, that was what they thought. If we survived this mission, I decided I would have a little discussion with Mr. Mulligan about some new topics he might add to Spy Battle class.

There weren't many options. I had no weapons and, even if I did, both of my hands were busy gripping the zip handle. As I mentioned, I am not very good with Jedi mind tricks, although there were a few points in this mission where I sure could have used them. About the only advantage I had at that moment was the element of surprise. So, I decided to use it.

With the shadows only twenty feet behind me and gaining fast, I turned my body to face them and hit reverse on my zip handle. The handle jerked in my hands as it reversed direction and carried me toward the agents.

The distance between us closed fast. It would be only seconds before impact. From their speed, I could tell that the agents had no idea that I had stopped and reversed direction. If they had known, they probably would have slowed down, and my plan wouldn't have worked. But they seemed so intent on going fast that they didn't even notice, and they certainly didn't slow down.

A split second before impact, the darkness around us was suddenly replaced by the light from a nearby office window. Everything became visible for just an instant.

It was perfect timing. I hit park on my zip handle, locked it in place on the zip line, and gripped it tightly. Then, I raised both legs, feet first, toward the oncoming agents, and prepared to kick with all the force in my body.

Waiting for impact was like watching a movie in slow-motion. Three agents came toward me. Lenny was in the lead, followed by Agent Blue and another of the agents from the roof. There was no sign of Isabel.

They came toward me fast and had little time to react. With surprised, almost panicked, expressions they scrambled to switch their handles to reverse mode. Their handles jerked and shook as the gears tried to slow and switch to reverse. But it was too late. They were too close and moving too fast.

The soles of my feet landed directly in Lenny's chest, knocking the wind from him and bringing him to a split-second stop. Agent Blue and the other agent slammed into him from behind, creating something like a squished Lenny sandwich.

I probably should have left it at that. I had slowed them down, and a wise move would have been to escape with a turbo boost on the zip handle.

But I didn't feel wise. I felt angry. Angry at Lenny for betraying the Institute. Angry at Agent Blue for chasing us all over the city. Just plain angry. Adrenaline surged through my body as my legs recoiled and I couldn't resist the temptation to kick Lenny one last time.

It was a mistake.

Just as my kick landed, Agent Blue's arm reached over Lenny's shoulder and grabbed hold of my right leg. His grip was like a vise around my ankle. I kicked and squirmed and twisted, but he didn't let go.

I was stuck.

It took Lenny only a few seconds to recover from my kick. I was surprised he recovered so quickly. And I was even more surprised by his first punch. It landed squarely in my gut, knocking all the air out of my lungs.

"Just give up the chip," Agent Blue said as I hung from the zip handle, gasping for air.

Lenny swung at my face with his right arm, and I blocked his punch with my left. The zip line swayed back and forth in the sky as Lenny and I traded blows, him swinging with his right arm and me blocking with my left.

I knew I couldn't let it continue. There were three of them and only one of me. And, as Mr. Mulligan would have said, fighting while dangling from a zip line probably wasn't "the best use of a spy's skills."

Lenny's punches were coming consistently now. Always with the right hand, always aimed directly at my head, always blocked by my left arm. It was like he had only one move and he was going to keep trying it over and over until it worked.

The thing about his one move was this: every time he swung with his right arm, his body twisted to the left, leaving Agent Blue's chest completely exposed.

It was the perfect opportunity. I tightened my grip on the zip handle and, as I blocked his next punch with my left arm, I stiffened my right leg, twisted my body to the left, and directed a kick past Lenny and into the chest of Agent Blue.

It was a total surprise to Agent Blue. One moment he was holding one of my legs in his hand, watching Lenny try to punch me. The next moment he was watching my left foot plant itself directly into his chest.

The force of the impact made Agent Blue lose his grip on the zip handle and on my leg. In just a split-second he was falling toward the ground. It was like that moment in a movie when the villain finally gets what is coming to him and everyone in the movie theater applauds. But I didn't feel like applauding. I didn't feel happy or relieved or victorious. As I watched him fall, the only thing I felt was sad. After all, I didn't want Agent Blue to die. I didn't wish that for anyone. All I wanted was for him to let me finish my mission. That and, you know, stop trying to take over the world.

Fortunately for Agent Blue, Lenny was one of those kids who wore pants that were about three sizes too big. The kind of pants that sagged down around the hips and looked like they were about to fall off. The kind of pants that, in a stroke of good luck for Agent Blue, were the perfect thing for a falling agent to grab.

Agent Blue didn't waste the opportunity. As he fell, he reached out and grabbed Lenny's waistband. It was a smart move, but the thing about pants like Lenny's was that if you pulled on them hard enough, they would come off. That was nearly what happened when Agent Blue grabbed them. The force of his weight on that waistband pulled the pants down around Lenny's hips and all the way down his legs. Agent Blue was left dangling from pants that hung from Lenny's ankles.

Lenny didn't seem bothered by the fact that Agent Blue was hanging precariously from his pants. He didn't seem bothered by the fact that his pants were around his ankles, revealing the brightest blue *Finding Nemo* boxer shorts I had ever seen. He didn't even seem bothered by the fact that I had planted both my feet into his chest, leaving him gasping for air.

Something else seemed to be bothering him. He had a worried look on his face as he tried to get words out. "Nate—" he said before gasping for breath. "Nate—" Another gasp. "Don't trust—" he said before his voice was replaced by sustained gasping and coughing.

I couldn't stay and wait for him to catch his breath. I had accomplished what I wanted to: I had slowed them down. It would take at least a few minutes for Lenny to catch his breath and for Agent Blue to climb up to his zip handle. That was enough of a head start for Lucy and me to get away, and I wasn't about to waste that head start waiting around listening to Lenny.

Still, as I hit forward on my zip handle and sailed away from the enemy agents at full speed, I was struck by the look on Lenny's face. He looked worried. Not for himself. Not for Agent Blue. For *me*.

I didn't have time to process that look of concern on Lenny's face. I was too busy hurrying to join Lucy on the next building.

"What took so long?" Lucy asked as she stood on the roof of the building waiting for me. "I have the next line set up, but I didn't want to leave without you."

"Well, let's just say I had some business to take care of," I said, acting cool.

"Business, huh?" Lucy laughed. "What, like did you stop to check your portfolio or something?"

I blushed in the darkness. "Um, well, actually, Lenny and the other agents were following us. I had to slow them down."

The smile drained from Lucy's face. "Following us? Like on the zip line?"

I nodded. "Yeah, I slowed them for a few minutes, but we need to hurry."

Lucy was suddenly a whirl of activity. Within seconds, she had us attached to a new zip line, and we were sailing through the night sky at full speed.

It took us only a few minutes to arrive on top of the Empire State Building. It wasn't an easy journey. Lucy led the way, creating a path of zip lines from building to building, like a giant dot-to-dot across the New York skyline. I followed closely behind, my arms aching with fatigue as I gripped the zip handle and wished for the journey to end.

Once there, we perched on a narrow ledge above the observation deck. I figured we were on about the 103rd floor, and from there we had a sweeping view of the city. The city lights twinkled in the darkness, and the cool nighttime air felt refreshing on my face. I could have stayed there for hours, but I knew we had to get moving.

Far behind us on the zip line I could see three shadows moving slowly toward us. The enemy agents had recovered, and they were still following us.

"The university is that direction." Lucy pointed. "I can probably get us close, but I don't want to use the TL yet, or I will lead them right to the building. What do you think?"

I looked around. We needed a way to slow them down, and I was pretty sure my feet-to-the-chest trick wasn't going to work again. And anyway, we needed more time than that. We had to delay them for at least fifteen or twenty minutes to give us enough time to complete our mission. Otherwise, they would simply follow us to the server room and undo whatever we did.

"This will do it," I said. One of the pipe joints along the side of the building was caked in a gooey sort of substance that looked like half-dried finger paint. "We'll just put this gunk on the zip line after we pass through. It'll slow them down."

"Yeah, it'll probably ruin their zip handles," Lucy said as she shot a new zip line toward a building a few hundred yards away and far below us. "They'll have to get down to street level to follow us, and by then we'll have enough time."

I nodded and began collecting the gunk. Without a place to store it—our mission packs didn't come with gunk-collection equipment—I did the only thing I could think of: I rubbed it down the front of my shirt. It stuck to my shirt in clumps like sticky clay.

Lucy was already attached to the zip line when I turned to follow. I moved slowly for the first ten feet, leaving the zip line completely clean. I wanted them to start out on what they thought was a clean line. Then as we moved slowly down the zip line, I coated the line behind us with the sticky, gooey, clay-like gunk. When I finished, about a twenty foot section of the zip line was coated in the stuff.

"Okay, that should do it," I said as I turned to Lucy. "Let's get out of here at full speed."

"Roger," Lucy said with a chuckle as she zipped away.

For at least a few minutes, I thought it had worked. We were making good time as the downward slope from the Empire State building helped accelerate our pace along the zip line. I trailed directly behind Lucy, holding the strap on her mission pack as it rested securely on her back. Staying together made things go faster. It also made me feel safer.

As we reached the mid-point between the two buildings, I looked over my shoulder to see if our plan had worked. Sure enough, I could see three shadowy figures dangling helplessly and still on the zip line far behind me. They were stuck. And we were moving.

I felt pride and relief at the same time. Our plan had worked. Our mission was on track. It would soon be over. It was time to adjust the scoreboard. Syndicate 2, Nate and Lucy 3.

That was when two events changed my mood immediately.

The first event shouldn't have surprised me, but it did. Without any warning, and without a sound, the entire city suddenly went dark. Imagine staring at a star-filled sky that suddenly changed to black. That was what it felt like for Lucy and me. Every building and every light, except for the headlights of cars below, suddenly disappeared. The sky above the city was bathed in total darkness.

Of course, we knew that this was part of the Syndicate's plan. We had overheard the agents talking about it. It meant their plan had started. They had taken control of the city's power. The next step would be an attack on the Institute itself.

The second event was even more surprising and more serious than the first. I had just recovered from the shock of seeing all the lights go out, but I was still confident that our mission would succeed. After all, we didn't need lights to complete our mission. We were spies. We had night vision.

That was what I was thinking when I felt the zip line jerk.

The first jerk was gentle, like a soft tug on a friend's sleeve. The second jerk was stronger. And by the time the third jerk came, it was with a ferocity unlike any I had ever felt. It was like a shark suddenly had hold of the other end of the zip line.

Behind us, I could see that the agents had made their way back to the building. At least that part of our plan had worked. We had slowed them down by forcing them back onto the building.

At first I thought they were trying to shake us loose of the zip line. I tightened my grip on the zip handle and on Lucy's pack, which I still clutched with my other hand. I was determined not to let go, even if it took all my strength.

But it soon became clear that my strength didn't matter. They weren't trying to shake us loose. They were doing something else, something I should have expected but didn't.

They were cutting one end of the zip line.

And by the time I realized what they were doing, it was too late.

It was hard to tell what had happened at first. After all, the city was dark. But after a split second, it became very clear indeed. One thing about the human body was that it pretty much knew when it was falling from hundreds of feet in the air. And if my body didn't know, my eyes quickly told me as I looked down and saw the headlights of the cars below getting closer and closer at a faster and faster pace.

Lucky for me, Lucy was a fast thinker. With less hesitation than I usually took before eating a chocolate-covered pretzel, Lucy reached into her pack and opened up her tunnel chute. I tightened my grip on her pack as the chute opened in the air above us. We gradually began to slow until we were falling at an easy pace toward the street below.

Once again, I was thankful for the tunnel chute. It wasn't designed as a parachute, we had never tested it as a parachute, but at that moment it was my favorite parachute of all time. As far as I was concerned, it belonged in the parachute hall of fame.

As we sailed slowly toward the street below, I thought of the traffic and pedestrians, and the people in the darkened office windows that surrounded us. If the lights had been on, and if people had looked above the streets of New York City, they would have seen quite a sight falling from the night sky: a sixth-grade boy hanging from the backpack of a sixth-grade girl, both of them suspended from a red parachute with "LOL" painted in bright yellow letters.

But as far as I could tell, nobody was looking as we drifted toward the sidewalk. That was probably because the power outage caused the traffic lights to stop working and, within seconds of the power going out, there had been a traffic accident on the street below us.

All eyes were focused on the smoking cars as Lucy guided us expertly to a soft landing on the sidewalk.

"It's this way," Lucy said as she stuffed the tunnel chute into her mission pack. "I guess we stay above ground. I don't trust the tunnels, do you?"

"No way do I trust those tunnels." I imagined the underground city below us crawling with enemy agents and I shuddered. "It's going to feel weird going on a mission above ground, though."

"Okay, we'd better hurry," Lucy said. "If the lights are out then the plan is under way. We don't have much time. Spy specs on."

That was how we proceeded to our final destination. Two agents, two pairs of spy specs, and two sets of eyes scanning the crowd on the sidewalk for any sign of enemy agents. There was no longer any confusion about what we were trying to accomplish. Our mission was clear, and soon everything would be over.

But I wasn't thinking about those things as we walked toward the university. My mind was occupied with a simple question that had occurred to me when we were chased up the elevator shaft. It gnawed at me as we sailed through the city on zip lines. And it started to really bother me as we fell from the sky onto a darkened New York City street.

It was a simple question, really.

Where was Isabel?

12. THE ENCOUNTER

The question lingered in my mind. *Where was Isabel?*

I wasn't sure why. It was like that time I forgot to put my Gadgets paper in my backpack when I left for school. I knew the whole day that something was wrong. It bugged me during Codes class and all the way through lunch. I couldn't say what was bugging me until I stepped into Gadgets class and realized what had happened. That was when I felt my heart drop into my shoes.

I tried to focus on the mission. The fate of the Institute rested on it, and so did the lives of our fellow agents and families. It was the only thing I should have been thinking about.

Still, as we walked toward the university, I couldn't help wondering what had happened to Isabel. She was at the building, long before we escaped on the elevator. But that was hours ago, and we hadn't seen her since. *Where was she?*

The university campus was blanketed in darkness when we arrived. We were wearing our spy specs with night vision activated, but evidence of the darkness was everywhere. People on the sidewalks stumbled through the dark with their arms stretched in front of them like zombies. Signs that normally would have been bathed in light faded into the dark nighttime background. Even the skateboarders moved slowly, with their arms stretched in front of them.

Poppleton left us clear instructions in the secret message:

> TAKE CHIP TO THE UNIVERSITY.
> COMPUTER SCIENCE BUILDING.
> ROOM 506.
> SERVER ROOM.
> PLACE IT IN THE COMPUTER.
> LUCY WILL KNOW.

Unfortunately, we had no idea where the computer science building was.

"How are we going to find the computer science building now?" Lucy asked.

I thought for a moment. We had a pretty good lead on the enemy agents. They didn't know exactly where we were going when they cut our zip line, so they probably weren't that close. "I think we use the TL."

"You mean tell them where we're going?" Lucy said, exasperated.

"Well, sort of," I said. "Maybe just search for the building. We can find the room once we get there without using the TL. That way once we get in and get out they won't know where we placed the chip."

"Got it," Lucy said as she entered the building information into her TL. "Okay, this way."

It took us only a few minutes to get there. When we arrived we found the building completely deserted. The stairs were empty, the lobby was empty, and the hallways were—you guessed it—empty.

On the one hand, an empty building was good for our mission. It allowed us to move quickly. Plus, we didn't need to worry about who was watching us.

On the other hand, it was creepy.

"Okay, let's get this over with," I said as we climbed the stairs to the fifth floor.

"Yeah, it's like scary soup in here," Lucy said.

Room 506 was at the end of a long hallway. We hurried through the unlocked door, anxious to complete our mission. We probably had less than ten minutes. It depended how fast Agent Blue, Lenny, and the others ran once they saw our TL search location come through.

I was immediately surprised when we entered the room. I had expected to enter an office with only one or two computers. It would have been easy to tear the cover off one or two computers, find a motherboard with a chip missing, and insert the chip in the empty slot. Presto, our mission would have been accomplished. But I saw immediately that we were dealing with something completely different.

"Uh-oh," Lucy said.

"Yeah, I'll say."

We stood in a room the size of a basketball court. Hanging from the ceiling in rows were long baskets holding computer cables. More computer cables than I had ever seen. Miles of computer cables, in fact. And every few feet, a line of cables stretched down from the ceiling to the floor, creating dozens of cable columns scattered throughout the room.

Arranged in neat rows, with a small walkway between each row, were hundreds of computers. Many more

140

computers than we had expected. Many more than we could have examined in one night. Certainly more than we could have examined before Agent Blue found us.

My shoulders slumped. "We don't have time for this. They'll be here soon."

Lucy nodded. "He must have given us a clue. No way would he expect us to take apart all these computers."

"Yeah," I said as I replayed the message in my head. "But the only thing he said in the message is 'LUCY WILL KNOW.' What does that mean?"

"Dude, I don't know," Lucy said. "Right now I don't feel like I know much of anything."

We started walking down the rows. The computers all looked the same: small black rectangles with cables coming out of them like roots and branches. Each one had a small panel of lights on front of it. As I walked through the rows, I realized that the computers were on. The lights blinked occasionally and every so often a gentle whirring sound came from one of them.

"Backup power," Lucy said as she noticed the same thing. "They must be on backup power."

"That's good," I said. "At least if we find where to put the chip it will be in a computer that actually works."

We approached the last row of computers, and I started to give up hope. I began to understand that phrase, 'searching for a needle in a haystack.' There were too many computers and too little time. I felt like surrendering.

That was when we saw it.

Taped to the top of a computer in the back corner was something that Lucy couldn't have missed. It was a small green piece of origami folded in the unmistakable shape of Yoda.

"That's it!" Lucy yelled as soon as she saw it. "Origami Yoda!"

Anyone who knew Lucy—*truly* knew her and didn't just know her name—knew that origami in the shape of Yoda had a special meaning for her. It was the first shape she learned to fold, from the back of that book, *The Strange Case of the Origami Yoda*. She loved that book. And every other book in that series. She once spent an entire assembly whispering to herself about Darth Paper. That made some heads turn.

There was no doubt that this was the computer we were looking for.

Relieved, I was.

I scrambled to remove the cover. The bolts had already been removed and the cover slid off in seconds. Inside were several rows of thin green plastic rectangles, each one with dozens of chips attached.

It didn't take long to figure out where our chip belonged. On one of the plastic rectangles, in ink that glowed fluorescent through my night vision setting, was a small but carefully drawn smiley-face. Poppleton, or maybe it was Professor Wilson, had thought of everything.

"Right there," I said as I pointed. "Be careful, the electricity is on."

Lucy pulled the chip from her pocket and, being careful not to touch anything else, gently pressed it into position.

The computer came to life immediately. The lights on the front began flashing and a gentle whirring sound came from inside. It was the sound of the hard drive booting. Seconds later, every computer in the room came alive with lights and beeps and whirring sounds. The room filled with a symphony of hard drive sounds and a sparkling show of computer lights. It lasted for a full minute. Then, as quickly as it had started, it gently calmed, leaving a room that was quiet and calm.

The overhead lights flickered on at the exact moment the computers calmed. Through the windows, light came from streetlights and the windows of other buildings. The air around us began moving as ceiling fans and the central air conditioner came on.

It had worked. If the power was on, the virus must have been destroyed.

Soon, I was sure, we would receive a message from the Institute that everything was back to normal and that our mission had been successful.

"Nate," Lucy whispered as she grabbed my arm. "We need to get out of here. We can't be caught or they'll find the chip."

I nodded. I didn't know exactly how the chip worked, but I agreed with Lucy that we couldn't risk letting the Syndicate figure out where we had placed it. If there was even the slightest chance that they could reverse the process, I didn't want to be responsible for showing them the way to the chip.

There was another reason that I was anxious to get back to the Institute. I wanted to feel safe. I had spent the entire day hiding, running, climbing, and hanging my way through danger. I wanted to rest in a secure place. And with Agent Blue, Lenny, and the other agents roaming the streets looking for us, I wouldn't feel safe until the hatch door at Red Station was locked tightly behind us.

We left as quickly as we had come, rushing down the fully-lit hallway and descending the stairs two at a time. I felt an exhilarated sense of calm as we strode through the lobby. We had succeeded in our mission. The Syndicate had been defeated. The Institute and our fellow agents were safe. All we had left to do was to get back to the Institute without being caught.

That was when we heard the gentle voice coming from the lobby in front of us.

"I always knew you two were the clever ones."

I knew who it was without even looking. I would've recognized that voice anywhere.

It was Isabel.

She stood alone, between us and the only exit, with her hands on her hips and a sad look on her face.

"Isabel," Lucy said. "It's over. The virus has been destroyed."

"I wish it were over," Isabel said as she shook her head. "But I need you to tell me where you put the chip."

"But don't you see?" I said. "There's no point now."

"Oh, there's a point," Isabel said. "I can reverse it if I find the chip. Just tell me where it is."

"We'll never tell," Lucy said as she crossed her arms in front of her chest. "Never."

Lucy was acting brave, but she knew as well as I did that if Isabel captured one of us we may not have a choice. She had ways of getting information when she wanted it. That was one of the things eighth graders learned at the Institute: techniques for making people give up secrets.

Isabel knew all the techniques.

I didn't know any of them, and I preferred to keep it that way.

"Teamwork," I whispered to Lucy as I slowly walked to my right, circling around Isabel until Lucy and I stood on opposite sides of her. Two enemies were harder to fight than one, especially if they were coming from different directions. That was one thing I picked up from observing Mr. Mulligan's spy battle class.

"Nate, I know all the tactics you do." Isabel slowly rolled her eyes. "Do you really think the two targets strategy is going to work on me?"

I shrugged. "I don't really know any other strategies."

Isabel laughed. It was just a normal eighth grader laugh, not an evil double agent laugh. It made her seem less threatening, but only for a moment. "I like your attitude. You know, I thought about recruiting you instead of Lenny. But it wouldn't have worked. Too loyal. Lenny was easier."

"Let's get this over with," I said as I lunged toward her. I was done talking. It was a waste of time, and it was giving Agent Blue and Lenny time to get here and back up Isabel.

Isabel ducked as I swung a clumsy punch at her head. She followed with two quick punches to the gut that sent me staggering backward.

Lucy was more creative. She faked a right-handed punch, and then unleashed a powerful left-legged windmill kick. It was the sort of kick that would have sent Isabel flying backward if it had landed.

But Isabel saw it coming. She caught Lucy's leg in mid-air, twisted her own body to the left, and used the force of Lucy's kick to throw her across the room.

Lucy landed with a thud against the far wall. She lay there grimacing for a moment before slowly picking herself up, clutching her sides in pain.

I didn't have time to worry about Lucy, though. Isabel turned and attacked me immediately with a volley of blows that forced me to stumble clumsily backward in an awkward retreat.

Surprisingly, my awkward retreat was actually pretty effective. Perhaps one of the advantages of, you know, "observing" spy battle class was that I never actually got a chance to practice any attacking or counter-attacking moves. It made me unpredictable, and it certainly wasn't something an agent like Isabel would have trained for. So stumbling backward and aiming a few poorly-executed stomps at Isabel's foot worked better than even I would have imagined.

Isabel paused for a moment with a surprised look on her face. Her volley had been intended to finish me off, yet I was still standing. For the first time, I began to sense that her confidence was shaken. She was clearly more skilled than I was. But I had the advantage of being unpredictable.

"Just give up," Isabel said as she turned to face me. "Save yourselves the trouble."

I could tell she was stalling. She wanted the fight to last as long as possible to give Agent Blue time to show up and help. We couldn't let that happen.

I lunged toward her, landing a punch on her for the first time and managing to trip her with a kick that sent her to the ground. But she quickly recovered and came back at me fast with a series of kicks and punches and chops that sent me careening into the wall.

She took two steps toward me, preparing for a final blow.

Only Lucy's quick thinking saved me.

"Hey, what's Poppleton doing here," she said as she pointed to an empty spot behind Isabel.

Isabel whirled around to look, giving me all the time I needed to make a crawling escape.

"Clever," Isabel said as she recovered. "But being clever won't be enough. Not with my training."

I began to suspect that she was right. Yes, there were two of us and only one of her. But that wouldn't matter unless Lucy and I found a way to combine forces. Somehow we had to find a way to attack her at the same time. Or, at least, occupy her attention at the same time.

We were on opposite sides of Isabel, circling her slowly and waiting for her to attack, as my eyes locked on Lucy's for just a moment.

It was all the time we needed.

We exchanged quick half-nods. Yes, they were half-nods. There was no time for full nods. We were busy. Maybe you noticed?

Then I took a half-breath. Yes, it was a half-breath. Again, I was in sort of a hurry. I would have plenty of time later for all the full breaths I wanted. At least, I hoped I would.

With Isabel pausing to decide which of us she wanted to attack next, I made her decision for her. It took me only four running steps to reach her, and I covered the distance in less than a second, swinging both arms like windmills.

Baffled, Isabel parried each blow and countered with graceful but strong kicks to my sides. Only a few of my blows landed on her. All of her kicks landed on me, and they didn't feel good. Within a minute, I had crumpled to the ground at her feet, helpless to defend myself.

Isabel stood over me, preparing for one last kick to finish the job. She hesitated for only a moment, but it was plenty of time for Lucy to start her attack.

"Hey, Isabel!" Lucy yelled.

Isabel turned to face her but she was too late.

Lucy had launched the somersault-spin kick and was already flying through the air, in mid-somersault, preparing to land a two-legged kick in Isabel's chest. I can only imagine what Isabel might have been thinking as she turned to see the soles of Lucy's feet coming toward her.

She might have been thinking that she should have expected the attack.

She might have been thinking about a plan to avoid the full force of Lucy's kick.

She might have been thinking that she made a mistake in joining the Syndicate.

Whatever she was thinking, it didn't make a difference. It was the chance I had been hoping for. Ignoring the pain in my sides and the fatigue in my arms, I pulled myself to my hands and knees and positioned myself directly behind Isabel.

Lucy's kick landed with the force of a piano falling from the sky. Isabel staggered backward, just as I thought she would. While she had been watching the soles of Lucy's shoes get closer and closer, I had positioned myself on my hands and knees directly behind her.

So, as she tried to take a staggering step backward to steady herself, she tripped over me and fell with a thud to the ground.

Isabel groaned and clutched her chest as she tried to catch her breath. She was injured and hurting but looked like she would recover. We didn't have time to wait around to help her. We had to get back to the Institute.

So, with Isabel's groans echoing through the lobby and hallways, we darted out the front door in a full sprint.

"How do you want to get back?" Lucy asked as we ran across the lawn in front of the computer science building.

"There!" I pointed to a round metal grate in the middle of the street. "That's the lid to a maintenance shaft. We'll go that way."

The prospect of climbing down into the subway tunnels didn't excite me. In fact, it sort of frightened me. But I knew that was the fastest way back to the Institute. The sooner we could attach ourselves to a zip line and get home, the better.

We climbed down the maintenance shaft and hung from the ceiling before dropping onto the subway tracks. As we landed and activated our night vision, I heard Isabel's footsteps on the street above.

She was following us.

"Quick, the TL," Lucy said as we landed. "She knows where we are, anyway."

I nodded as I dialed in our location. "Over there! There's an access point over there."

We slammed against the door of the access point without hesitating. We had no time to waste, and we learned our lesson in that first tunnel. These old doors needed force applied to them or they wouldn't budge. The door swung open instantly, and within seconds we were safely inside the old tunnel with the door secured behind us.

"Isabel will find it just like we did," Lucy said.

"I know, but we have a head start. This tunnel inter-sects the main Red Line right up here," I pointed to our right. "She won't be able to catch us."

The hinges of the door creaked behind us as we sprinted toward the Red Line. We ate up the distance between us and the intersection as fast as my brother Charlie ate Oreos. Honestly, if there had been an Olympic event for running through a tunnel and getting ready to attach to a zip line, I'm pretty sure Lucy and I would have made it to the finals.

"Get ready," I said as we approached the intersection at a full sprint.

The narrow zip line hung from the ceiling, as if beckoning us to hurry.

Lucy was leading the way, with her zip handle in one hand, prepared to attach to the zip line in one fast motion. I was following one step behind, ready to do the same.

Just as I was adjusting my steps to prepare for a giant leap onto the zip line, I noticed Lucy sliding to a stop in front of me. It was the last thing I expected, and for a split-second I was baffled.

Then I saw the boots.

They were hard to see at first. Just the very tip of a pair of boots peeking out from behind the corner of the intersection, as if the people they belonged to thought they were hidden but had miscalculated by just an inch.

I scrambled to stop, but my momentum carried me forward into Lucy's back. I crashed into her and sent both of us tumbling until we ended up sprawled motionless on the ground in the center of the intersection.

I stared, unblinking, as I tried to regain my breath. It had been a hard fall, and I still wasn't sure exactly what had happened, but I noticed a few things in my field of vision right away.

I noticed the smooth walls and gleaming metal beams of the main Red Line tunnel.

I noticed the zip line suspended securely from the ceiling.

I noticed Lucy struggling to sit up.

I also noticed something else. Something—or, rather, some*one*—that I had hoped never to see again.

It was Lenny. And he was looking down at me with the oddest expression I had ever seen.

"What took you guys so long?"

13. THE END

Seeing Lenny's face and hearing his voice filled me with rage. My heart pounded faster and my hair stood on end. The last person in the world I wanted to see was the double agent who had betrayed us. I was about to jump up and attack him when a familiar face emerged from the shadows at the edge of the tunnel. It was Red Station Chief.

"Okay, let's get back to the Institute. It isn't safe here," he said as he motioned us to attach our handles to the zip line.

"But ... but ... " I stammered, pointing to Lenny. "He ... "

My voice trailed off as I struggled to find words to match my thoughts. *Lenny was a traitor! Didn't Red Station Chief know? Had Lenny somehow tricked him? Was Lenny planning a secret attack from inside the Institute?*

"No time for talking," said Red Station Chief sternly. "Get yourselves attached and let's go. This place is crawling with Syndicate agents."

Yeah, I wanted to say, *and one of them is standing right next to you!*

I could tell Lucy wanted to say the same thing, but the urgency in the station chief's voice made us pay attention. We attached ourselves to the zip line behind

Lenny and within seconds the four of us were zipping toward the Institute at full speed.

Poppleton was waiting for us with the hatch door open. "Quickly, quickly, get inside. That's it. No time to waste."

As Red Station Chief locked the hatch tightly behind us, a wave of relief spread through my body. Locked safely inside the Institute, with Poppleton and Red Station Chief to lead us, all the pressure of the mission drained away. It was over. At least, most of it was over. One loose thread kept me from relaxing completely: Lenny.

"He's a traitor!" I blurted out, pointing at Lenny. "He's working with the Syndicate!"

Lenny just stared at me with a smile on his face. It wasn't the sort of smug, devious, mocking smile that I would have expected from a traitor, though. It was a different kind of smile. Sincere. Relieved. Happy.

"Well," said Poppleton, "He was, and he wasn't."

"Sure seemed to me like he was working with them," Lucy said. "The dude chased us around the city all day!"

"I did, that's true," Lenny said. "But I was only doing it to figure out their plans, and to help Poppleton figure out who the real traitor was."

"That's right," said Poppleton. "Lenny was acting as a triple agent. You see, I suspected for a long time that we had a traitor in our midst. Too many missions were being compromised; too much information was being discovered by the Syndicate. I knew it was no accident."

"It was Isabel all along," Lenny said as he shook his head. "I didn't want to believe it, but she recruited me this morning and I went along with it to follow their plans. I couldn't be sure the two of you would succeed."

"Yes, you may have noticed that Lenny has been acting rather, um, *unpredictable* lately?" Poppleton asked.

"Like a jerk sometimes, you mean?" Lucy asked bluntly.

"Well, yes. I suppose. But it was part of the plan. I knew Lenny wasn't the double agent, so I told him months ago to start acting a bit, well, *unreliable* is the word I think I used."

"He figured if I acted like I couldn't be trusted, the double agent would try to recruit me to work for the Institute," Lenny said. "And it worked."

"I have to say, I'd hoped it wasn't true," Poppleton said. "Isabel. I still have trouble believing it."

I thought back to the events of the day. It was true that Lenny had never been the one to actually threaten our mission. He had been tagging along. And what was it that he had said when I was kicking him up on the zip line? *Don't Trust*— I suddenly realized that he had been trying to warn me about Isabel.

"We shouldn't dwell on this too much," said Red Station Chief. "We need to recognize these kids for their successful mission."

"So true. So true. We were this close to having the Institute overrun by Syndicate agents." Poppleton held his forefinger and thumb an inch apart. "You know, the virus had taken down our computers. Another hour and our security measures wouldn't have worked any longer."

"What about the list?" Lucy asked.

"Safe," Red Station Chief said. "But just barely. There are a lot of agents—and a lot of agents' families—that owe you two a lot."

"Let's go," Poppleton said as he ushered us to the doorway. "We can discuss this in detail at the mission evaluation assembly. Your parents will be here soon. Basketball practice is scheduled to end in a few minutes."

"Yep, it's all clear," Red Station Chief said from behind his computer screen. "Syndicate agents are pulling back. I don't think we have to worry about them."

I was about to ask what had happened to Professor Wilson. But before I could even ask, the door swung open and revealed him standing in the hallway with a grin on his face. He looked so much more relaxed than the last time I had seen him that I barely recognized him.

"Good work, kids," he said with a smile. "I wasn't sure you would pull that one off."

"What happened?" Lucy asked. "Did they capture you?"

"Ha!" Professor Wilson said with a chuckle. "They only wish they had caught me. I might be an old man, but I still have some tricks up my sleeve. Or, rather, gadgets on my feet."

We watched as he pressed a button on his shoe and a set of small wheels popped out of the sole.

"This was my last project in Gadgets Lab," he said. "I call them shoe-skates. They were pretty creative thirty years ago. Now, they're nothing special on most days.

But this morning, they were enough to get me away from those agents and safely behind these walls."

"Well, just barely," Poppleton said. "They sure wouldn't have been enough for you to complete this mission."

"Oh, heavens no!" Professor Wilson said. "That's what kids are for."

"That's right," Poppleton said. "Anyway, time to get moving. Your parents will be waiting."

A sense of satisfaction swelled in my chest and spread throughout my body as we walked down the narrow passageway from Red Station to the stairway. Lucy and I had completed a Level One mission. We had saved the Institute and our fellow agents from destruction. For now, at least, the Syndicate had been defeated.

Without even thinking about it, I took a full, deep breath and, as Lucy and I entered the elevator to exit the building we exchanged slow, deliberate, completely full nods.

The door closed behind me and I was alone in the elevator listening to the familiar computerized voice that I had heard every day since I started going to the Institute.

"Eyes closed," said the voice as the air in the room swirled.

"Eyes open," said the voice as a narrow beam of red light scanned across my eyes.

"Stand still," said the voice as the metal ring lowered from the ceiling, moving from my head to my feet and back up without ever touching me.

"Arms in front, palms up," said the voice as the palm scanner shone blue on my palms.

"Thank you for your service, Agent Nate Fischer," said the voice as the elevator rose to street level and the doors opened into the cool evening air.

It might have been my imagination, but I thought I sensed something different in the computer's voice, like a new sense of respect for my spy skills. Perhaps the computer had already heard about our successful mission. Or, I guess, it might have been just my imagination.

"See you tomorrow, Nate," Lucy said as she walked down the steps and climbed into her parents' car.

"See ya," I said.

Charlie was sitting in the back seat of the car reading on his Kindle when I got in. He didn't even look up. Clearly, *he* hadn't heard the news about my successful mission.

"How was practice?" Dad asked, as if this had been just another ordinary day. Clearly, *he* hadn't heard about my successful mission, either.

"Okay," I said.

"How was school?" Mom asked. Clearly, *she* hadn't heard about my successful mission, either.

"Good," I said. It was the most boring description I could imagine of the most exciting day of my life.

I wanted to tell them about being chased through the tunnels and the subway system.

I wanted to tell them about zipping across the New York City skyline at night.

I wanted to tell them everything.

But I knew I couldn't. I had to keep The Secret.

So I kept my thoughts to myself and tried not to think about the mission. For the entire car ride home, during all of dinner, and all the way through family game night, I focused—or at least tried to focus—on other things.

I had never been so excited to go to my room for the night. Alone and safe in my reading tent, I began to imagine what I would say at the mission evaluation assembly the next day. The thought of all those agents listening to Lucy and me describing our mission made me feel proud. I couldn't wait for that assembly, or to hear what Poppleton would say about us.

Even more than that, I couldn't wait for the next mission.

Before I rolled over and went to sleep, I updated my mental scoreboard one last time.

Syndicate 2, Nate and Lucy 4.

Game over.

NOTE FROM STEVEN STICKLER

Dear Reader,

I hope you enjoyed reading about Nate and Lucy's first mission. If so, here are a few things you might consider doing next (check with your parents first, though; keeping secrets from your parents is not cool):

1. Post a review. Take a full breath, give a full nod, and post a review on Amazon, Goodreads, or wherever you enjoy sharing your thoughts on books. It's fun, and it will help other readers decide whether they want to read this book.

2. Tell your friends. Because book suggestions should be shared among friends just like potato chips, good music, funny stories, and chewing gum (actually, I do not recommend sharing chewing gum; that's just gross).

3. Consider reading my other book. You might like it.

Thank you for reading,

Steven Stickler

ABOUT STEVEN STICKLER

Steven Stickler is no rocket scientist. He will never be confused with a professional athlete. He is not (despite widespread rumors) the actor who played Cousin Oliver in The Brady Bunch, nor was he a guest drummer for the Beatles during a brief period in the mid-1960s. He is something completely different: a writer. He began writing when he was five years old and, due to an oversight by those in positions of authority, was never told to stop. He lives in the great Pacific Northwest of the United States, where he enjoys exploring the outdoors with his family and, of course, reading at least one book by Dr. Seuss every year.

Steven Stickler lurks in some of these places:

Email: sticklersteven@gmail.com
Facebook: https://www.facebook.com/AuthorStevenStickler
Blog: http://stevenstickler.wordpress.com/
Twitter: @StevenStickler

ALSO BY STEVEN STICKLER

The Absolutely Amazing Adventures of Agent Auggie Spinoza

Auggie Spinoza is a ten-year-old boy with a secret: he is a special agent who can travel through time. Now, he finds himself locked in a desperate battle against evil forces trying to change the course of history. To defeat them, Auggie must pursue a dangerous quest to find a set of mysterious clues hidden in the past.

With the help of a clever new friend and advice from a cast of famous characters with names like Jefferson, Darwin, and Plato, Auggie fights to fulfill his destiny and save his world from ruin. Along the way, he learns the importance of thinking clearly and shows the awesome power of a code-breaking, book-loving, time-traveling ten-year-old with a talent for being in the right place at the right time.